You can't trust anyone these days...

That is when Avi makes his last mistake. He hands me the gun while he arranges the wires.

When the car engine starts, he raises his head and I raise the gun and point it at my soon-to-be-late partner. His dark eyes stare at me quizzically.

"You know one thing that bothers me," I ask, "why haven't you asked me my name?"

He smirks. "I know who you are. I don't need your name."

Tales of Mystery and Suspense

Published by 53rd Street Publishing

Logo image by:

Engraver | Dreamstime.com

Ebook ISBN 978-1-927621-17-2
Trade paperback edition ISBN 978-1-927621-16-5

Cover image © Photowitch | Dreamstime.com

Dedication

As always, my love and devotion goes to Rita for everything that makes this life worth living.

Table of Contents

Introduction

Between these pages you will find five unique mysteries. One involves a private investigator framed for murder, another tells the tale of a writer walking into the middle of a robbery at a casino during a blackout, while another relates the story of an elderly man forced to confront his own fears.

The mystery genre has a wide range of styles and characters that reflect how we as human beings cope with crime and criminals. What these stories represent is a range of styles and characters that I hope readers will find entertaining, suspenseful, and satisfying.

If you have feedback to offer I welcome you to contact me on Facebook or Twitter.

Happy reading.

R.G. Crossley
August 2011

Boomerang

Serendipity.

Life is filled with moments of serendipity.

After all my life's work was as much a surprise to me as anyone. After serving in the first gulf war, I found killing people was my destiny. Being paid large sums of money for doing something you love is the bonus.

Now here I sit in smoky pub of a cockroach-infested hotel on the downtown eastside of Vancouver, sipping a warm beer beside one of the cockroaches. This particular cockroach appears to be the most hard luck thief you have ever met. I'm wondering how I was going to slip away.

I couldn't very well walk out the front door because I had stirred up the cops like an angry hornets nest after I had dotted the "I" of Mrs. Reginald Phillips.

My signature is to shoot the target once in the head — what I call "dotting the I" —with a soft-tipped bullet. This creates maximum splatter as the bullet spreads out after contact and blows a large hole in the back of the skull creating a shower of brain matter and blood. This causes witnesses to react with horror and panic allowing me time to escape. The challenge is you have to get really close to the target.

Mr. Phillips was the Donald Trump of Vancouver; he owned most of the glass and steel monuments-to-better-living that decorated the downtown skyline. The guy must have a net worth of at least a billion bucks.

Unfortunately, for Mrs. Phillips, 'ol Reggie wouldn't cooperate with the nastier elements of the construction industry. While it is not my place to speculate about the reasons for the elimination of a target, I read the newspapers like everyone else.

Two days after a very public dispute with the heads of the construction unions an envelope arrives in my drop box filled with cash and surveillance photos of the target. (My fee is usually twenty thousand dollars.

The unnamed client paid me twice my usual fee because this was a high profile job. It would also allow me to lie low on a foreign beach for an extended luxury holiday.)

At first, I am doubtful I can make this a clean kill and consider refusing the job. I knew 'ol Reggie boy had his own security goons so I'd need to plan this one carefully. After all, I want to get away from it all to enjoy my fee.

I follow the Phillips around town for two months prior to the hit in order to document their every move. Finally, an opportunity presents itself that will be perfect. I decide to make the hit on an upcoming Wednesday.

Frankly even I am surprised when my plan plays out exactly as I envision it.

Reggie and his wife — whose name was Veronica, if I remember correctly, or was her name Victoria? Not that it really matters — will be at the grand opening ribbon cutting ceremony of his new luxury apartment tower. There will be a large crowd comprised of his employees, and local newspaper, radio, and television news people. A perfect crowd of unfamiliar faces I will be mingle with to get in close. I even have a fake press pass to get past security. I love the thrill of a close kill.

Boomerang

My scouting report indicates the egotistical bastard forces his employees to attend his openings to applaud his growing empire and increasing personal wealth. To any of his employees who refuse to attend he gives them their walking papers. Charming...

I plan to disguise myself as an old man. My father was a movie makeup artist. He taught me his craft when I was a teenager with the hope I would eventually join him in the family business. Unfortunately, Dad and Mom died in a car crash just before I left for the gulf.

My disguise work is perfect. Wherever he is, I'm certain Dad's proud of me.

After mingling with the crowd, I get close then, with my homemade silencer affixed to the barrel of my untraceable pistol, I dot Mrs. Phillips "I".

As I anticipated, the resulting pandemonium covers my escape to a nearby alley I selected in advance. It is here I discard my disguise and dispose of the gun in a dumpster then disappear into a pre-selected pub.

So here I am, sitting next to Avi Kumar who reeks of mold. He sat down at my table after I arrived. And he's talking my ear off.

I nod my head as if I'm listening to his every word while taking the occasional sip of the warm sleeve of beer that long ago lost its foam cap.

My eyes scrutinize the dimly lit pub from the plain black plastic dust-covered fixtures hanging low over the round terrycloth covered tables to the vacant faces of the working class customers. The place reeks of beer, stale cigarette smoke, and sweat. A real working man's bar. My kind of place.

The bartender is a raven-haired woman with a lean figure. She appears to be no more than thirty-five, but her hard features give her the appearance of a weather beaten sailor. Her emotionless gaze suggests she has fought off one too many drunks in her day. Our waiter's large belly hanging over his belt tells me he has consumed generous quantities of this establishments wares.

My plan is to leave after a couple of hours and take a bus home. For now I am listening to the felonious exploits of a two-time loser.

Avi's dark skin is marred with an angry scar that runs down the right side of his face from beside his right eye to his wide chin.

He sports the baggy clothing gangsta look that is the rage in the music videos; his baldhead appears oddly shaped like one of those misshapen pumpkins left over after Halloween.

Avi's not the master criminal type. He tells me he held up a laundry mat on his last job. He did two years less a day for the big soiled diapers caper.

I am surprised he is telling me any of this crap. I might be a cop for all he knows.

Yeah, the guys a real super villain. Where is Superman when you need him?

It was a good thing I had dropped my .32 caliber Ruger in the dumpster in the alley two blocks away. If I still had my gun I would definitely have a hard time resisting the urge to dot this guys "I" free.

"I have a great job planned and I need a partner...you wanta come with me?" says Avi his words slurred from the two beers he has inhaled since he sat down.

I am about to refuse this excellent career opportunity when I see a gaggle of uniformed cops accompanied by two plain-clothes men, who have to be Phillips security linebackers, come through the twin oak doors that led to the sidewalk.

A cloud of steam follows them in and I smell the rain that has started to fall outside.

It's time to leave.

"Sure, Avi, I'd be happy to," I say sounding cheery. For a second I think I may be laying it on a little thick, but my doubts are quickly erased when a sloppy smile crosses Avi's face and he grunts. "I gotta a car parked nearby," he says.

I slap him on the shoulder. His faded blue jean jacket is soft under my touch. "Great. Why don't you and I talk about the job on the way?" I indicate the uniforms making their way through the pub. They stop occasionally asking for identification from patrons at random. The low murmur of conversation masks the questions-asked-and-answers- given. The place is packed for a Wednesday night, but since we're far enough back in the gloom, they don't notice us yet. Unfortunately this won't last long.

Avi glances at the cops and nods. "I hate pigs," he mutters.

He and I stand as one and head for the rear door that leads to the alley. Once outside I consider breaking his neck and leaving him. But since I am no longer in disguise, and since the waiter that served us has seen us together, I decide to wait.

We make it to his car, a rusting late model Chevy, and I offer to drive. Given his unsteady feet the cops'd stop him if he drove. I think 'ol Avi has had a snoot full before he got to the pub.

As we drive on the rain-slicked streets, he instructs me to head for Southwest Marine Drive. Avi says a new Happy-Mart has opened in that area. He tells me his second cousin went to high school with the night manager, a fat wimp named Albert. Fat Albert is going to be taking the afternoon bank deposit to the bank an hour from now at ten o'clock. His plan is to jump Albert and steal the deposit.

I want to strangle this moron. Hasn't he ever heard of debit cards, credit cards, and checks?

He grins and says, "I know what your thinking... there won't be a lot of cash, right?" I nod but keep my eyes on the road, and the speedometer so I don't drive too fast. We don't need to attract unwanted attention from some eager cop.

He laughs, his arm resting across the back of the bench seat of his ancient Chevy, and says, "My cousin says half of their daily take is cash and they do twenty thousand per shift."

Ten thousand? Cash? Hmmm...if it's true then I will be able to extend my holiday.

I glance at Avi and wonder about the shape of the splatter pattern his misshapen head will make when I blow a hole through his head. No one is gonna miss this guy.

"You help me with the job and I'll cut you in for twenty-five percent."

"A quarter share? That's all?" I try to sound indignant because I know I am going to get a one hundred percent share.

He laughs again. "My cousin gets twenty-five and you get twenty-five. I get half because...." he pats his jacket ..." I have the gun."

***

We arrive with half an hour to spare. I get us some coffee in Styrofoam cups from a nearby 7-11 and we sit in the parking lot waiting for Albert. Finally, when my patience is waning, he appears.

Albert is wearing a white dress shirt and navy windbreaker and black-rimmed glasses, and yes, he is a *very* fat man. Beads of sweat dot his wide pale forehead. Tucked under his right arm is a brown bank deposit bag.

Avi and I get out of the Chevy and walk toward Albert who is concentrating on fishing in his windbreaker pocket for his car keys. He is standing beside a late model steel gray Toyota Corolla.

My temporary partner in crime moves behind the fat man and pulls out a pistol, which he sticks it in Albert's back. For his part Albert looks like he's about to have a heart attack he's bathed in sweat and trembling. I detect the odor of urine. Great. The fat boy's bladder has let go.

"Move and I'll kill you," says Avi. He says it with sufficient menace I even believe he might kill the poor guy.

I step up and yank the deposit envelope out of Albert's pudgy outstretched hand. I glance at Avi who has a sneering grin on his face and nod.

We turn and start back for the Chevy.

"Hold it!" says a voice behind us. I freeze while Avi turns the gun held level in his right hand. With distain evident in his voice Avi says, "It's okay. It's only Albert."

I turn around to see Albert is holding a snub-nosed revolver in trembling hands. He looks like he's going to shake the thing apart. Is he serious? He's going to get himself killed.

I decided I had better stop this thing before it gets messy. "Com'on, Albert. Drop the gun or ..." I indicate my partner, "... he'll shoot you. Do you want to die for the Happy-Mart deposit?"

Albert's eyes are wide with his face contorting with inner confusion. "Do you guys know me? Do I know you?"

The air erupts with a gunshot. Albert's white shirt explodes with a flood of red and he drops to his knees the gun leaving his hand to clatter sharply across the pavement. The now very dead Albert falls on his face with a soggy smack.

I look at Avi as if to ask him why he shot fat Albert. He shrugs. I don't care either. Happy-Mart will find another night manager.

"I guess we better get another car," he says. I realize the Chevy wasn't really his car. Interesting, the guy really did have an actual plan. I gain a new respect for my temporary partner.

I nod in concurrence. After scanning the parking lot for cars that are easy to steal, I spot a blue Ford Taurus with a plastic cross hanging from the rearview mirror that will fit the bill nicely.

We head for the car. We break in easily with a lock pick Avi's carrying. He bends down to get underneath the steering and commences to hot-wire it like a pro. Hmmmm...the guy really does have some marketable skills. Too bad he's going to be dead sooner than later

That is when Avi makes his last mistake. He hands me the gun while he arranges the wires. When the car engine starts, he raises his head and I raise the gun and point it at my soon-to-be-late partner. His dark eyes stare at me quizzically.

"You know one thing that bothers me," I ask, "why haven't you asked me my name?"

He smirks. "I know who you are. I don't need your name."

I love the smell of burnt gunpowder. The pistol jerks in my hand and the back of Avi's head explodes; a shower of blood and brain matter covers the driver's side window behind him. After smacking the window his head slumps forward his chin resting on his chest.

Odd...the bullet should have gone through his skull and shattered the window. I hold the pistol up in the dim light coming from the street and notice the serial number is filed off. My heart freezes. The .32 Ruger ... with my fingerprints all over it. My specially made soft tipped bullets would not be able to penetrate the window

I feel the urge to laugh aloud at the irony, wouldn't the cops love to get their hands on this weapon.

The gun used to kill three other people tonight has my fingerprints all over it: Mrs. Phillips, a fat Happy-Mart night manager, and the late Avi Kumar, super criminal. Avi must have found my gun in the dumpster before coming into the pub. No doubt a happy coincidence for him.

The Taurus' engine suddenly dies and a voice comes from the car radio. "Don't move. This is the police. You've stolen a bait car. The doors are locked. You cannot escape."

I stare at the boomerang Ruger. Once the cops test the gun and find out where it was used tonight

***

Serendipity. I wonder how Avi knew who I was? And I wonder if life has more surprises in store for me. I raise the pistol to my temple. My only hope is there is a beach on the other side ...

Cape Disappointment

1

HANDS TREMBLING, BEN HARRIS, RE-OPENED the manila file folder lying on his cigarette scarred oak desk in the squad room.

He'd been afraid to open it since the Captain dropped it on his desk, six hours ago. The other six homicide detectives were gone for the day, their stale fast food containers still filling the room with greasy fried odors mingling with the already dusty atmosphere of the squad room.

He was alone.

The patter of rain striking the single paned windows echoed in the quiet of the room competing with his rapidly beating heart.

The metal accordion lamp sitting in front of him, near the edge of the desk, cast a yellow pool of light over Kelly Harris' dead eyes staring back at him from the autopsy photo.

Her chalky pallor, blue lips, and battered face failed to reveal the woman who he loved in a previous life. No one knew the bitch the way he did. No one could.

Her body had been fished out of the near freezing water that morning near Cape Disappointment, where her killer had dumped her.

The report said she had not been dead prior to being placed in the gray waters of the rock strewn bay. The coroners' report, in the folder opposite the photo, made it clear she didn't die of hypothermia.

The rocks, with their sharp edges and unyielding steadfastness, had punished her face almost beyond recognition. Looking at the photo he would've recognized her anywhere.

He recalled her full hips and ample bosom lying next to him in bed. And her soft hands caressing his back as they slept curled next to each other in a fetal hug protected and warm. A lot of time had passed.

His dark navy suit pants rustled softly as with his right hand, he attempted to snap off the lamp switch.

His hand shook so violently he had to use the ebony fingers of his left hand to steady himself and take in a few deep breaths. After placing the file folder back on the green blotter covering the burn marks on his desk the trembling finally stopped.

After pausing a few seconds to regain his focus, he managed to push the red slider across the switch assembly thereby interrupting the connection. The white forty-watt bulb dimmed, and then went out. Only the remaining heat from the blub served as reminder it had it had been on. That too would soon disappear.

He rose from the ancient tan oak chair, its crushed burgundy cushion doing little to protect his growing secretarial spread. He pulled his matching suit jacket off the chair back. Once the jacket covered his sweat stained white shirt he loosened his red striped power tie around his thick neck and sighed. A deep weariness had invaded his bones. He was so tired.

Wind swept raindrops struck the windows covered with chicken wire mesh in sufficient force to remind him of a war zone. In his youth he'd fought wars not crime.

He picked up the manila folder then walked toward the wood framed glass door leading to the hallway and the old Otis elevators beyond.

What little light there was coming through the fogged glass acted as a beacon allowing him to find his way through the darkened room.

Near the door there stood a large shredder over which, fixed to the wall, was a black sign, with large white print. It read: No investigative files must leave the squad room. All top-secret files must be shredded.

Underneath some joker, probably his partner Miller, had stuck a yellow post-it note with the words, *Investigative files are secret files*. The *are* was underlined.

Ben smirked as he placed the file in the shredders feeder and hit the green button on the side. The machine sprang to life with a roar filling every wall of the quiet room then quickly consumed the file contents and all.

He snapped the shredders button to the off position and the room returned to a quiet calm.

No one would be investigating this case. Kelly's gone, plain and simple.

The glass in the door rattles as he opened it. He glanced down at the thin strips of paper in the bin beneath the feeder and realized she wasn't worth it. No one was.

The door closed behind him and his footsteps faded into the distance.

2

Rose Thomas studied the dancing snowflakes through the small window of the lumbering 747 as it neared the end of the runway. The city spread out below her lay under a blanket of white. The streets and byways cut black lines like squares on some fairy tale giant's blanket. It felt good to return to Vancouver.

She clipped the fine tipped ball point pen's plastic clip into the rings that ran up the spine of the blue cardboard-protected, ninety-eight cent binder resting open on her lap.

She glanced down at the numbered, finely etched script on the nine by seven paper with a sense of satisfaction. Her list was ready. Now she was eager to get started.

Jack, her husband of ten years, seated in the seat beside her, was certainly useless when it came to decision-making. Her role in life was to be the decision maker in their family. She wore the metaphorical pants.

She smiled to herself as it occurred to her how long she'd been away. New husband, new job, all had changed in the intervening years. She relished the thought of catching up with her old friends, Liz and Carla.

She looked at Jack with his hands gripping the seat rests with an intensity so strong he might break off the arms any second.

He may be a coward, but he was her coward and that's what counted. She could keep any man under her thumb, not like some women she knew.

Naturally, she hadn't given him any say in making this trip, even though it was taking time away from her writing, and drained much needed funds from their bank account. A small town cop's salary didn't go far these days. He would just have to work some over time.

Her royalty checks went into her private account, to cover off her writing expenses. Not that they payments were that much, but after this convention that would change.

She'd long considered it odd that her publisher never sent her on book tours. Her first poetry anthology went to print during her college days, some twenty years previous. The book sold well, and finally her second book of Poems was about to be published. Friends who read her work assured her she was a damn good poet.

"You okay, Jack?" He wasn't.

The sweat reeled in sheets off his forehead, and his normally pale face was flushed and blotchy. Through eyes squeezed tight, like he was being treated to a dance on hot coals, he nodded and said nothing.

She knew he hated flying in any kind of plane, big or small. But then he had always been a baby about such things.

Good thing she was here to look after him.

Initially, when she'd told him she was going to Vancouver for the convention, his fear had evaporated until it dawned on him he'd have to fly to get there. His initial reaction was like that of a lap dog, its tail wagging furiously, begging her to take him along for the ride.

As he'd explained, his blue eyes sparkling with delight, he hadn't been to Vancouver in years. In fact, he'd only been here during one cross-country road trip with his family when he was ten. Reluctantly, she agreed to let him come with her.

The plane's tires squealed as they came into contact with etched surface of the runway. The sound echoed through the skin of the aircraft. The plane swayed slightly from side to side as it settled nose first then began its roll out. Rose was certain Jack would scream if the movement from side to side continued.

The four-turbo fan jet engines attached to the football field sized wings roared in the cabin as the pilot changed the levers to the reverse thruster position. Simultaneously they were pressed back into their seats as the pilot stepped hard on the brakes in order to impede their forward momentum. Rose felt the tension ease in her husband as the plane began to slow.

Rose could see the flaps were now fully extended out the small, porthole sized window, next to her.

Jack sighed as the single breath he'd been struggling with for the past several minutes, escaped between his dry lips. Sweat stained his yellow golf shirt, and his short, dark hair, normally combed neatly into place, laid pasted flat against his forehead.

Rose reached into her shiny black, plastic coated, purse on the floor underneath the seat in front of her extracted a wad of white tissues and handed them to him.

The plane continued on its drive to the terminal bouncing and shuddered its way across the runaway.

Jack grinned at her, obviously relived at being on sacred ground again. He mouthed a thank you, as he mopped the excess moisture from his head and neck.

She acknowledged him with a regal tip of her head, though her thin lips remained pursed, as if she were a school marm acknowledging her student.

The co-pilots voice echoed over the speaker system welcoming them to their destination, and to issue the usual de-boarding instructions to the passengers.

They were to get off on gate 23 then proceed to the baggage area where their luggage would be unloaded on carousel 23A. Ellen made a quick mental note of this information then looked about her to make sure she had every thing. Yes, her checklist was complete.

The plane stopped and everyone around them started standing to open the overhead bins and retrieve their valuables. They pushed over one another to drag down their particular bag or jacket from the bin. The petite oriental lady next to her prattled on in Chinese to the lady across the aisle, they were obviously traveling together, though neither of them had said anything to each other for the entire flight.

Jack and Rose were located in the center and window seats, he in the center near the rear of the cabin, so they would be among the last off. Rose decided to wait calmly for their turn while Jack began to fidget uncontrollably. In his view the thing was a flying bomb with wings waiting to happen and he couldn't wait to get to safety.

With the rapid fire words of the little Chinese ladies still permeating her nostrils, and the strong smell of garlic, left by the man seated in front of them, she gave the all clear signal to her husband.

Not needing further encouragement, Jack leapt from his seat, like a rabbit in heat, and hurriedly grabbed their black leatherette over night bag, and her lap top case, from the overhead compartment.

He wrestled them to the aisle seat as she undid her seat belt. She prided herself by following instructions to the letter.

Always keep your seat belt fastened until the plane comes to a complete stop at the gate.

These were standard instructions after every flight, and pretty clear ones at that. It bothered her sensibilities when other people ignored the rules. Therefore, she made it her life's ambition to follow instructions, just as an example for everyone else. Jack would sometimes insist on gently teasing her about her obsession, but she insisted it was what made her feel complete.

After Jack moved out of her way she shifted across the row of three seats from where she sat moving toward where he'd been standing. Her pudgy fingers grasped the orange and gray cushions of the seat backs in front of her to steady herself. Her gray, low rise loafers, with the rubberized soles and simulated leather uppers, made a soft shushing sound on the pale blue carpet of the plane's deck as she moved.

A person of her size was physically challenged by the cabin configuration most airlines insisted upon, which often made getting out of these narrow seats difficult, but not impossible. She longed for them to wake to her disadvantaged group.

Corporate thinking, not customer comfort, paid the bills something she could readily identify with, but was still miffed about.

Jack stepped back as Rose stepped into the aisle and ran her bloated hands down the sides of her forest green pant suit in a losing attempt to smooth out five hours worth of wrinkles. Jack, who was obviously feeling a lot better, grinned at her in his lop sided way.

"We made it," he said.

"Jack, do you always have state the obvious? Pleeease…" She rolled her eyes and stepped past him headed for the front of the cabin. She could feel the heat of his eyes on her as she walked away, but she knew he'd never say anything about more it.

3

Kelly tied the clean white apron over her pale peach colored uniform, and then pushed the stray strands of sandy brown hair behind her right ear. Stray hairs had again broken loose from the hairpins. She took a deep breath, just as she did everyday, then walked out of the combination change room, women's washroom into the staff common area in the back of Willie's Family Restaurant.

Her plain white nurse's shoes made a soft shuffling sound on the burgundy tinted cement floor as she hurried down the corridor.

She passed the dishwashers work area where a new guy, whose name escaped her, was sliding a plastic tray full of dirty plates standing on their edges like a row of soiled wheat into the automatic dishwasher. The rattle of the plates echoed through the confined space of the common area as he forced them inside then, using the handle on the side, brought down the aluminum walls of the cover around them and pushed the large green start button attached to polished solid steel work counter between them.

The array of chemical smells mingled with food smells of all descriptions in this area of the restaurant. This rarely made the dishwasher a popular guy.

She felt her skin crawl as the latest unshaven loser winked at her as she passed by. With a cigarette dangling from between chapped lips, and the greasy shoulder length trails of hair resting on his narrow shoulders, he wasn't the worst horror that Armstrong had hired. At least he didn't make the effort to comb some of those slick strands over the top of the large bald spot on top of his head like the last one.

Along the opposite wall from the dishwasher's station was a row consisting of six shiny steel fridge doors, each the dimension of the average sized man.

She recalled her revulsion when she had first thought about the fact you could store a six-footer in one if you needed to, and not even have to break the legs, as she'd heard morticians sometimes did with dead bodies to get them to fit in standard sized coffins.

She could see Mr. Armstrong, surrounded on two of the four walls of his small six by five workspace, sitting in his office, his smooth hairless scalp titled forward as he concentrated on the documents in front of him.

She tapped lightly on the hollow wood door, once. No answer. Twice. Finally he spoke up.

"Yeah. What the hell is it?" he said, the annoyance evident in his voice.

He pressed forward into the desk as she, barely missing his wheeled chair swung the door open to his cramped office. She secretly enjoyed making him have to press into his desk with his ever-growing girth making it more difficult with each passing week. Soon he'd not only get a red line across his belly, due to the force he'd use to avoid being hit by the door, but he'd get the door up his ass. Little pleasures, you took them where you could get them. This was a gift.

A deep furrowed brow and angry brown eyes greeted her. When he saw it was Kelly his face changed to a sunny expression, and his yellowed teeth showed from beneath his thick, dark mustache.

It was one of those bushy kinds of mustaches she'd didn't think anyone had worn since the seventies.

With his wide, soup-stained tie, and the polyester navy pants he wore every day to complete his ensemble, he looked like a throw back in time. Given his attitude toward women, was not such a stretch.

"Kelly, what a nice surprise. I didn't think you'd be on shift today."

"Huh, I'm not actually scheduled to work today, sir. I switched with Alice. I need the money."

She kept her eyes focused on his desk so she didn't have to look directly at him.

She didn't want to risk catching his eye thereby running the risk of forcing the wrong idea into his psyche. The last thing she wanted was him to think she was interested, which she most certainly was not.

There were unsubstantiated stories circulating about Mr. Armstrong, and she wasn't about to take any chances they might be true.

When the door opened a momentary look of dismay crossed his face, and then changed to what he must've thought was a reasonable facsimile of Romeo.

In his fucking dreams.

"Yeah, I guess that would be alright."

Kelly nodded then closed the door. She smiled to herself as she walked away. Changing shifts with someone was against the rules, and one she'd just broken and gotten away with.

Armstrong's door suddenly flung open and he stuck his head out. "I'll be out later, if anyone comes looking for me." She nodded, knowing she had dodged the bullet.

Feeling lighter inside she walked toward the double hinged door with the glass inset, at eye level, in the center, a feature designed to allow both the waitress' inside and outside to see each other coming. This little safety item helped avoid collisions, and workers comp claims.

After stepping aside, to allow Kay come through the door gripping, with two hands, a plastic bus tray loaded down with glasses, plates, of various sizes, and cutlery, she entered the customer area of the restaurant ready to take on another day among the living.

4

He slipped away with the intention of leaving Rose to enjoy her four to six afternoon nap in privacy.

Jack gingerly began to ease the door closed, using the burnished gray metal handle, to suite 1407 until, with a sharp click the latch caught. The Astoria Hotel is the finest of moderately priced flophouses in the center of town. Through the heavy pine door he could hear her regular, loud snoring that rattled the strongest of windows. She'd be asleep for a while yet.

He turned and started down the dimly lit hallway, which snaked around a corner out of his field of vision. The pot lights overhead created a trail of spots like breadcrumbs along the plush ruby and indigo carpet.

He cringed at the sight of then flowery wallpaper, which lined the walls. The blue, pink and yellow daisies were the gaudiest things he'd ever seen. Naturally, Rose liked it.

He followed the path laid before him until he returned to the bank of elevators from earlier when he'd carried their luggage from the lobby.

One pot light flickered as he passed like some seventies discotheque lighting system resurrected from obscurity just for him.

It made him think about Kelly and how she'd looked back then, before he'd left to become a cop in Toronto. Those were good days. Fun days.

The urge to dance, screw, and snort anything that was placed before him had given way to responsibility. Rose had made sure of that. She was organized and made his life easier every day.

He stepped into the elevator car and found himself alone, facing a perfect picture of himself. He pressed the lobby button and the doors slid shut with a resounding thump as they made contact. The car began to move.

He gazed at the middle-aged man with the receding hairline in front of him. The belly was a little softer and his rugged physique of twenty years ago was just a memory.

He held his breath and pulled his paunchy stomach in just as the bell, indicating the elevator was stopping to load passengers, sounded. The cars jerked to a halt and, after a momentary pause, which provided him the opportunity to let out his breath. He stuck his hands in his pockets in an attempt to appear casual. He didn't feel casual, he felt uncomfortable. He hadn't been to a bar in twenty years.

A young, well-scrubbed couple nicely dressed couple entered the elevator car.

The doors then closed once more and the elevator continued its downward journey. The glowing row of numbers over the doors inside the car lit up then went dark as they passed each floor on their way to the L. The lobby.

Why is this thing taking so long?

To pass the time, Jack studied the couple.

She was blonde, with the California thing happening. She wore wearing a blue and red striped tee shirt accompanied by tan slacks neatly pressed. The fresh razor sharp creases ran down both slim legs ending at the shiny knee-high heels showing from beneath the cuffs.

The guy, looking like a Back Street Boy, had on a jet-black tee shirt with the arms ripped off to the shoulder, and dark blue jeans. On his feet he wore white Nike's.

They each had an arm wrapped around the other, and were solely focused on gazing longingly into the each others eyes, ignoring him as if he was on another planet.

He concluded they were newlyweds. "Honeymoon?" he said his deep voice resonating off the constricted walls.

The guy, his face changing to one of anger with a speed which startled Jack, removed his arm from the woman's waist then stepped up to within inches of Jack's face. Jack could feel the heat of his breath and smell the steak he'd had for dinner.

"None of your fucking business." He pressed his index finger into Jack's chest, "old man," he added for emphasis.

Jack was tempted to take the guy down, but he restrained himself. The guy was right. It wasn't none of his business. "Sorry." He shrugged keeping his hands inside his trouser pockets.

Before the situation got out of hand the doors opened into the lobby and, after poking Jack's chest once more, again for emphasis, the couple exited the car together leaving him standing there alone. They whisked, like some human tornado, through the lobby then out the glass windmill doors into the street out front.

The man in front at him grunted at him then also entered the lobby disappearing toward the restaurant.

Jack gathered his composure, shook his head, and stepped out of the elevator. He cleared his throat. He'd never been so embarrassed.

He studied the front desk area until he spotted a sign hanging over an archway at one end of the large room. With tan colored wing chairs pressed into every available space. Large bay windows and orange clay pots containing a plethora of flowering indoor plants were scattered everywhere.

He sauntered past the large oak front desk, where a lone male desk clerk with blow-dried brown hair. His eyes followed Jack as came toward him.

He was on the phone obviously speaking with a guest whose needs had not been met, evidenced by the pained expression on the clerks face.

Jack smiled and nodded as he went by and the clerk smiled back weakly then continued to explain that what ever the problem was hotel policy.

Jack followed the signs until he found the hotel bar. Once inside he realized immediately it was unusual. The bar itself, a long expensive teak surface surrounded by high backed wicker chairs, had a view, on the wall behind, a swimming pool.

Not the full pool, just the under water portion, so that when sitting at the bar you had a view of the people swimming on the other side of the glass.

From his experience in interrogation rooms he recognized the glass was one sided.

Bar patrons could see in the water, but anyone swimming on the other side couldn't see inside the bar. It was truly unique in his experience.

Behind the bar stood the well-groomed bartender. His short wiry curls and pencil thin mustache made him appear more youthful than he probably was. He was standing with his hands behind his back wearing a navy vest, with the hotel logo on one side, a black bow tie, and a perfectly pressed powder blue shirt.

On his face was the most dazzling smile Jack had seen this side of toothpaste commercial. "Hello, sir," he said in a singsong tone. Jack thought the guy must be lonely or something, but he decided to play along.

"Hi, yourself. How about a beer?" Jack climbed aboard one of the wicker chairs to take it for a test drive.

"Certainly, any particular kind?"

"Naw, just whatever you have on tap."

The bar tender nodded then, after pulling down a pilsner glass from the over head rack, he drew a frothy glass of the amber liquid, then placed the glass in front of Jack on a cardboard coaster with the hotel logo stenciled across it.

Jack instinctively reached for his wallet.

"You a hotel guest, sir?"

Jack nodded. "Room 1407."

The bar tender wrote the number down on a slip of paper next to the register. "The charge will appear on your bill at check out time."

"Thanks." The bar tender nodded then turned and walked into the stock room, through a door to the left of the pool window, while Jack sat and stared at the blue water picture window before him fascinated by the mind of the person who'd thought this idea up. There was no one swimming at the moment, but Jack's imagination quickly ran away with him.

Then it struck him, as lightning often does on a clear summer day, hard to imagine on a November day in Vancouver. Kelly. An irresistible urge gripped him to call Kelly.

It had been far too long, and after all, how often would he be in Vancouver?

Stepping away from the bar, his beer half finished, he headed for the nearest pay phone. He was filled with child like excitement as his eyes searched for the familiar symbol on the lobby signs when he remembered Rose sleeping upstairs. She would never approve of him speaking with an old girl friend. He shrugged.

What the hell why not? What would it hurt?

5

Her tired muscles screamed in protest as Kelly stooped to pick up the community paper from the dusty burgundy carpet on the lobby floor of her apartment building. She made the additional effort because she liked to read the local stuff better than the morning tab or the pretentious afternoon edition, which billed itself as the source for news in Vancouver.

Exactly whose source they were supposed to be had always been a mystery to her.

On a sidebar on the cover she noticed there was an advertisement for the Vancouver Writers Convention being held at the Astoria downtown.

Folding the paper under her arm she scanned her copper colored metal mailbox and saw it was empty. For today at least there were no bills coming due, but there soon would be.

She walked to end of the carpeted hallway, which muffled her footsteps and climbed the two flights to her apartment.

Once inside she locked the deadbolt and slipped the light chain into place. Her mother warned her that single girls in the big city were often targets of the pervert league.

She doffed her white shoes by the front door, threw the newspaper on the over stuffed worn green couch pushed against the wall of the living room, then padded in her beige nylon'd feet into the kitchen.

The remnants of the beef stew she'd made for dinner for the following week still lingered in the air. The covered stone wear cooking pot sat in the old fifties refrigerator across from the white heavy ceramic sink.

The thing that made these three story walk ups popular was their character. The hardwood floors and expansive windows all around gave them a charm hard to find in this era of glass and concrete.

The answering machine blinked her so, after filling the tea kettle with water and placing it over a gas burner on the white ceramic stove, which she lit with a single turn of the third from the left of the solid black plastic knobs lined up across the front, she pushed the button to listen as she padded toward the bedroom with the intent of changing into her slob wear.

After she'd left the room she heard the machine beep then a voice from her past echoed down the silent hallway.

With her uniform dress bunched around her waist, revealing her black lace bra underneath, she raced back into the kitchen. With trembling hands she again called up the message.

Sure enough there it was him deep, sexy voice and all. Jack's here, in Vancouver, but he didn't say where exactly, he said he'd call her back.

Remembering his wife was a poet she retrieved the paper she'd tossed on the worn green couch when she'd entered and scanned the article about the writer's conference. The Astoria—he was at the Astoria. She looked out side the front window at the light snow falling and realized he was only blocks from where she stood right now. Her hands shook with anticipation.

6

Barney Armstrong watched Kelly walk away then turned back toward his desk. He'd been attempting to get into her pants since the first day he'd laid eyes on her, but so far he'd been unsuccessful. He shrugged and returned to re-read the letter sent to him from Shirley at head office.

The company logo glowed under the fluorescent lights directly over his small cheap laminated desk. It consisted of a gold W with two eagles surrounding it seemingly in worship of their founder, William "Willie" Woodson, a poor dirt farmer who'd gotten lucky.

Well today was Barney's day. His day to get lucky. His day to buy those expensive Italian leather shoes he'd had his eye on at the mall.

He pulled out a plastic red pen from white chipped coffee cup he used as a penholder and circled the most important paragraph of Shirley's letter.

The letter said she would be at the Astoria later this afternoon to discuss terms. If he didn't show the deal would be off. He glanced at the white faced electric clock with the black numbers and the thin hand slowly marching through the minutes and seconds to his future. Things were about to change for Barney Armstrong.

Easing back against the hard cushion of the worn gray secretarial chair he ran his hand over his damp baldhead. Glancing up Barney saw Albert, the new dishwasher he'd hired the previous Friday, share his toothless grin as he caught him standing, arms at his side, watching him. The reflective polished surface of the twelve-foot steel worktable was piled in front of him. Barney scowled at the lazy bastard and raised his right index finger to point at the mountain of soiled work that needed to be scaled within the next hour in preparation for the hungry lunch crowd.

The ex-con, still grinning like a schoolboy on the last minute of the last day of school before Christmas holidays, chuckled and nodded. Favors to old friends led to a road of sorrows. He shook his head at his own stupidity. Who was being dumb shit?

7

Precisely at six thirty Jack glanced at his Timex only to look up as Rose strode into the hotel restaurant. Her purposeful stride, navy blue pantsuit with the starched white shirt showing above the row of black buttons, which ran up the center, indicated to him she would all business tonight.

As was her practice her black handbag, the one with the metal clasp at the top, firmly secured of course, straps were slid down over her thick left wrist. Her expression behind her heavy black framed glasses told him she on one of her missions again tonight.

They'd been at the convention for three days now and she'd managed to piss off just about every editor and publisher in attendance. Of course, he dare not tell her retribution would make his life to now seem like a free ride.

She sat down the in the low backed wicker chair across from him and opened her notebook. He with the intention of limiting their conversation picked up the plastic coated menu and began to scan the pages for his choice of supper.

He'd told her before her nap time that he wanted to go out to eat. The food at the hotel, while it's okay, was beginning to taste a little bland to his pallet.

In Smith Falls he enjoyed the hunt for new, more exotic meals while on his meal breaks during patrol shifts. The restaurants in the surrounding communities had a wide range of foods he enjoyed. Japanese, Chinese, Greek, Italian all were available if you knew where to look. Rose had been raised in a British home where meat and potatoes were the staple of the diet. As usual his wishes were vetoed.

Rose checked off something in her book with her red felt tip pen as the waitress, a red haired woman, heavy around the hips, who wore too much red lip stick and with her face coated in a thick layer of white powder and orange rouge designed to highlight her low cheek bones, made her appear clownish which he didn't think was the look she hoping to achieve. This coupled with the lingering stench of cigarettes, which he'd unfortunately discovered when she'd recorded his drink order approached their table.

She must've sensed his discomfort earlier because her odor had changed and she now smelled of enough perfume to be employed in a French whorehouse mingled with the cigarettes it was an unpleasant combination.

Jack had to agree with Rose who wrinkled her nose as they woman approached.

"I'll have a glass of white wine," she said before the waitress could speak. "Chardonnay, not too dry." She cast her gaze on Jack who raised his glass of cheap blended Scotch to show her he already had his.

Rose smiled thinly then picked up her menu. The waitress nodded and started to walk away.

"We'll both have the broiled chicken, no potatoes, with extra vegetables. And make sure the cook knows that the vegetables were over cooked last night." Jack closed his menu and placed it on the table next to him. He didn't want chicken, but what choice did he have? None as usual.

"Yes, of course, ma'am." She gathered their menus then moved away, her pink polyester slacks rubbing furiously, before she became trapped by Rose's fastidious habits.

Little did Rose suspect the waitresses had taken to flipping coins to see who served the woman who needed the attitude adjustment. Tonight this waitress lost the toss.

Rose eased her body against the back of chair. Jack noticed it creaked slightly from the unwanted stress. He caught himself wanting to chuckle at the mental image on Rose toppling to the floor as the chair back broke from the strain. Instead he smiled, his unpolished coffee stained teeth providing his cover.

He glanced at the face of his watch again and saw it was nearing quarter of seven. Soon. Very soon.

"Going somewhere, dear," said Rose, her eyes cast downward focused on the pure white table cloth as snapped the white cloth napkin, with the finely stitched edges, across her lap with one theatrical flourish.

She then placed her elbows on the table and steeple her fingers in front of slightly bowed head, her dark eyes focused on his over the edge of glasses and waited for his response.

Jack felt his heart sink. She knew. That must be it, she knew. "Of course not, honey." He struggled with the words forcing a light tone into his voice.

She laid her fingers flat on the table, which she then smoothed her fingers moving outward from center toward the edges of the heavy linen tablecloth. "You don't look well. You should have a nap after dinner."

He nodded then they lapsed into silence. Rose slipped her handbag off her left wrist, where until this moment she'd keep it secure from all would be muggers, paranoia was her middle name, then unzipped a pocket on one side where she kept her grooming tools and retrieved a white plastic handled nail file. Carefully she laid the file flat on the tablecloth then, after ensuring the gold colored latch was firmly in place returned the purse to her wrist.

He was distracted watching Rose engaged in her grooming ballet. Her way of doing the most mundane of tasks had fascinated him for years.

It suddenly dawned on him he couldn't meet Kelly at their agreed upon place and time. When he had spoken with her on the lobby telephone after reading her message, the thirty-dollar tip to the desk clerk had secured his silence. They agreed they wanted it to be at the place where they had met all those years ago, Mustafa's Sahara Nights.

Unfortunately, the discotheque remained a fond memory of their youth. It was for the best and probably where such a place should exist.

It had gone out of business along with the best music of the '70's, as far as he was concerned, back in the early eighties.

The high-end tourist flea market that Robson Street had become with its designer outlet stores, espresso bars and trendy, here-today-gone-tomorrow restaurants had invaded the once, in his opinion, fun part of the city. No wonder the town had grown a rep for being the navy blue blazer amongst the cities in North America.

Instead, they agreed to meet at the coffee shop on Georgia Street at 7:30. It would be crowded with late Thursday night shoppers by then, and they would just be two people in a crowd.

Now he'd ruined everything. Kelly would think she'd been stood up just like the old days. The disappointment ate at him in the pit of his stomach.

He winced as Rose, who had taken her nail file out of her purse and started mindlessly humming to the beat of the elevator music coming over the restaurant's sound system. This was going to be a long, long night.

8

Kelly walked along the rain soaked pavement her full figure wrapped in the protection of the rain coat she'd purchased last fall in the men's only clothiers shop. It was black with gray trim and not a particularly attractive cut on a woman, but it was practical and that's what counted. The light snow of the last few days had changed to rain, a good thing, but the wind coming from the North Shore mountains still howled down the web of streets in the downtown core.

It was an easy walk from the bus stop on Burrard Street to the mall. She covered the distance in record time. He would be there waiting and she breathlessly wanted to get there as fast as her legs would carry her.

She arrived at the store at the appointed hour and scanned the street outside. With each passing second the anticipation and longing grew inside her. She heard he was a cop now and doing well. Funny how those things work out.

Finally he came into view his waist wrapped in a long black trench coat and a hat pulled down over his eyes to shield himself from the wind and rain.

They would go for a walk on the beach along the shore in West Van. The park near the lighthouse known as Cape Disappointment.

The park's name was due to the high number of deadly shipwrecks in that area back in the early part of the twentieth century. It would be deserted this time of day.

Her long dreamed of romantic evening with the one person that ever really mattered to her was about to become reality. She'd been with other men since those days, but this guy was special. It had taken over twenty years for her to realize it. Today her life would change. Forever.

9

Jack didn't try to call Kelly again. He'd done enough already, far more than he expected he would. There was never any answer at her apartment, and time was running out. Besides he didn't dare, with Rose watching his every move, expect for the four to six p.m. window when she had her daily nap. She was very precise.

Of course he also didn't have the courage to call Kelly again.

Kelly hadn't called back so he assumed he'd blown it, again, or maybe she'd lost interest, which was the more likely scenario.

Two days left of Rose's convention then he could go home where he belonged so who cared.

The feel of the steering wheel of the Chevy cruiser the town council bought for the department last year would be welcomed in his hands. Once he caught to odor of that new car smell he would be home, grounded for life. The sound of the three hundred and fifty cubic inch engine would course through his butt again.

Ten years to retirement would be his end. And his life with Rose would continue as before.

The red faux leather wing chair squeaked loudly as he shifted his weight to get more comfortable. The damn things were in reality medieval torture devices for guys like him with bad backs.

Glancing at Rose he saw the gentle rise and fall of her sleeping form underneath the teal bedspread. She's still asleep. Good he didn't need her bullshit on top of everything else. He was depressed enough.

Absent-mindedly he chewed on a fingernail from his right hand as he stared out the large picture window at the heavy raindrops falling from the low overcast. The larger clearer drops that were visible to the naked eye sped past on their journey to the red brick walkway he knew was far below his field of vision. The light from the room caused speeding to their inevitable doom. Much like his own life at this moment.

His glossy, black leather uniform shoes shone in the early evening light. It would soon be time wake Rose. His four to six respite was about to expire.

The city, once vibrant with life, looked dead to him. The colorful array of lights that met his gaze offered him

No joy.

Melancholy musings were interrupted by a burst of sound being emitted by the beige phone sitting on the brown laminate end table next to the queen bed. An identical end table stood on the opposite side to complete the set.

He couldn't will himself to move before Rose, rising on one elbow, her pink and blue flannel nightshirt rumpled from her involuntary night tremors picked up the receiver from its cradle.

"Yes," she said into mouthpiece, her voice edged with sleep.

Jack heard the echo of someone speaking then Rose sat suddenly bolt up right her eyes wide in wonder. For a second he thought she'd had a heart attack from the way her face drained of blood. The conversation finished with her acknowledging the caller and replacing the receiver with a sharp click.

She threw back the covers with her usual flourish and, after swinging her short legs so they were hanging above the charcoal gray carpet, and shifting her weight forward, she stepped barefoot onto the carpet next to the bed.

"I've got to get dressed. We have an appointment downstairs." Her voice was hard, and her gray eyes were filled with determination, her jaw clenched.

He stared at her unable to fathom what she was talking about. She walked toward the bathroom where she kept her makeup. "Why?" was all he managed to say behind her.

"There's been a murder."

Her voice echoed from inside the pale peach three-piece bathroom common to most hotels. The words hung in the air as he broke into a cold sweat beneath his navy gold shit, which he was now glad he'd put in place of the light red one. A sense of dread gripped him to replace his melancholy mood of moments before.

"What has this got to do with us? I'm on vacation, for God's sake."

"The cop said the dead person is an old girl friend of yours. Kelly somebody or other."

10

Ben sat with his black raincoat tossed across his left arm with his fingers locked together in his lap in the tight, ornately carved, low backed chair. It was the type of furniture he hated. It had wooden arms that cut into his side.

He distracted himself by studying the people going to and fro in the lobby. Being a trained detective he enjoyed studying the various people as they rushed by him.

His ability to make a living is based solely on his skill at observation, consequently. When the opportunity to practice presented itself he'd sit and watch people to see how they interacted with each other. It helped him keep his edge as detective.

The writer's convention currently going on at this hotel was a prime candidate worthy of his study. These people were unique.

Presently he had his eye on a middle aged bleached blonde wearing a green fake satin dress, an imitation fix fur slung around her neck, and a white floppy hat with an ornate pink feather sticking from the top.

Tethered at the double leash in her right hand were two miniature schnauzers. The leash had been shortened to restrict the dog's movements and prevent them to stray too far.

From what he could tell from the direction she was headed she was about to run headlong into the hotel manager. The manager's reaction at seeing her dogs should be educational and fun at the same time.

What would've been a very entertaining moment ended when Rose Thomas trailed by her husband, Jack, appeared from one of the elevator as it disgorged passengers into the carpeted lobby area. Being the only black man in the place made their recognition of him pretty much a given. Similarly their expressions told him they knew who he was.

Ben's round belly jiggled beneath his white shirt as he pushed himself forward with both hands to escape the grip of the prison he found himself in.

Many times he'd thought about offing the person who'd made these chairs. They were so lacking when it came to comfort or practicality. Of course, they also discouraged people from hanging around hotel lobby's creating problems for him and his brothers and sisters on the force.

He held his striped red tie down over his tailored navy wool suit as he stood to greet the Thomas'.

Jack Thomas held out his hand and his narrow face broke into a wide grin.

From his research at the station before coming to speak with them Ben knew Jack was a small town cop in Ontario, which made the news he had to deliver that much more complicated than he would've wished.

Rose Thomas however was another matter. Her thin lips and corpulent frame made her appear doughy. The heavy black frame of her glasses hanging off her long nose reminded him of his third grade teacher back in grammar school.

Apparently she was some kind of poet. Ben knew nothing about poetry or poets, but for some reason she looked every bit the part as far as he was concerned.

Ben held out his hand and after gripping Jack's found it was firm and solid. He did notice his hand was moist indicating he either sweat a lot naturally or was nervous.

Rose appeared somewhat indignant about having to meet with him.

"Perhaps we should go somewhere private?" said Ben casting his gaze on Jack.

Rose glared at him her eyes filled with rage. "I knew it. We could have stayed in our room and done this." Her tone said cold bitch and reminded Ben of his ex.

"Actually, a forensic team is going over your room as we speak," Ben said trying to sound apologetic.

"You think we had something to do with the woman's death. It was an accident wasn't it?" Rose folded her arms across the rise of her large breasts. Her white sport sock clad feet, sealed in green and gray plaid bedroom slippers, shuffled back and forth as she spoke.

"I didn't mean..."

"What are you saying?" Rose interrupted him. Her posture was straight and her green unyielding eyes focused on his black ones

Ben frowned, placed his right hand in his trouser pocket, and then changed gears. He decided to modify his tone and information sharing to elicit an emotional response, one he could weight and measure. The detection game was truth and dare. He'd used this technique many times to find the liar among the range of suspects.

In this case there were so many loopholes, and suspects, he knew it wasn't going to an easy case. This bitch was making it even harder with this attitude. If she wanted to dance then so be it, start the music.

He lowered his voice as he stared his face a mask of patience. "Mrs. Thomas, I am trying to eliminate suspects. True you didn't know the victim but you're husband did. At one time," he added.

Her eyes went wide and she turned to face Jack who visibly shrunk. The smile disappeared from the small town cop's features since the conversation had turned. Up to this point Ben thought he seemed to be enjoying his wife's antics now that her focus was off him.

Ben, watching the woman's face turn an unimaginable mixture of shades of purple and red before she would unload on the guy, decided he better in to save the poor guy's ass.

"At this point I also don't believe he actually did it. My suspects usually have far greater reasons for murder than unrequited love. Seeing as you're a writer this is a terrible clichéd idea don't you think?"

This appeared to stop her in her tracks. He'd hit her where she lived. Her ego wasn't about to be bruised. Of course she knew that old standby, and since her husband was a cop, the idea was unthinkable and even more of a silly notion.

Her pallor returned to its previous pale complexion as she thought about what Ben had just said. For a few seconds she stood still her face frozen with the expression of someone deep in thought, her eyes flitted back and forth (the wheels of her mind obviously turning.)

Finally she, her shoulders slumped ever so slightly, straightened her suit jacket, and after making an attempt to rip from her head one of the short mousy brown curls of hair hovering over her left ear, as if in some kind of bizarre torture ritual, she made up her mind. He thought for a second she might actually yank the curl, roots and all, out of her scalp like a cork screw if she pulled hard enough, but she managed to let her do live to fight another day.

"Is there anything else?" Her tone suggested defeat. It was clear the lady didn't enjoy losing.

"Yes, I need to talk to your husband alone."

Rose glanced at Jack then red faced, and still twisting furiously at the curl of loose hair, turned. She hurried away like Canada geese being chased by toddlers in some public park. With a flash of the green slacks he concluded no doubt part of an ensemble she disappeared into the restaurant.

Jack watched her go his face the symbol of calm. When she was out of sight he broke down and laughed. Tears streamed down his cheeks, and the no doubt hard won paunch of his stomach shook.

Ben smiled to himself. He and Jack had more in common than being policemen.

"Boy, you really showed her." Jack managed to choke the words out between guffaws.

Ben withdrew his right hand from his trousers. He reached inside his suit jacket pocket to pull out his notebook. He flipped it to a blank page and began to write something with a black and white ballpoint pen. As Jack watched Ben's actions his laughter subsided until he realized what this meant.

"You're going to arrest me aren't you?"

"Yup." Ben reached behind his navy suit jacket and pulled his metal handcuffs from the hidden pouch he kept there. Some guys liked to wear the pouch on their side he like to keep it hidden. In his opinion it was less intimidating and made soliciting much needed investigative information easier. Now he needed them.

The act of pulling back the jacket to revealed his gold detective's badge on the right front of his belt near to the left of the trouser pocket made the color drain from Ben's face.

Being polished to a high sheen the cuffs glowed in the late afternoon light streaming thought the double skylights forty feet overhead. Even in winter the sky would be sometimes bright from stray rays of sunlight that managed to escape through the overcast. Even on one those dull, gray Vancouver winter days.

Ben clipped the first ring around Jack's wrist accompanied immediately by the ratcheting sound as they were locked into place.

After getting Jack to turn his back to him, Ben slipped the other one around his remaining wrist. He then pulled the man's arms together in the approved position, slipped the end into the locking mechanism and completed the job.

He knew from his year at the Ontario police college in Brampton that he had little hope of proving his innocence. The evidence was purely circumstantial, but he realized he'd left a trail of phone calls, answering machine recordings and love notes a mile wide. He knew he didn't kill her he loved her.

By this time a crowd of curiosity seekers had gathered to watch. As Ben read him his rights his deep voice echoing on his unfocussed hearing Jack's bladder let loose with a flood of piss that soaked through his clothes to run down the inside of his pant legs.

Ben finished reading the warning and caution from his brown leather notebook then replaced it inside his jacket pocket.

As he led Jack away Ben heard a voice say, "Hey look, the stupid bastard peed himself." Followed immediately by gales of laughter.

11

Ben, having changed into tattered blue jeans and a white tee shirt, leaned back only to sink into the over stuffed couch facing the large picture over looking the harbor.

He shared his one room apartment with his cat, Jessie, a little white and orange tabby he'd found wandering the streets near his building some months before.

Jessie sat at his feet quietly licking her paws.

He lifted the cold beer can to his lips. After taking a swallow to cool his aching throat he set the can on the light colored pine coffee table. The unused cardboard coasters with little gold anchors imprinted on them sat unused stacked in the center of the table.

His empty gaze stared at the white, red, and yellow harbor lights that dotted the shoreline. Kelly was dead and there was nothing he could have done to prevent it.

Jack would be released tomorrow after the captain found the file folder missing. No evidence. No case. That was the rule.

He let the whisper of a sigh escape between his lips then reached for the beer can to take another blast. Oblivion had to be better than this.

For a second he wondered who had killed her.

He didn't care but the detective in him, that special something that made him the love to solve mysteries something that he was good at, begged to be let free. He suppressed the thought immediately.

She was a whore and deserved to be dead.

He'd been waiting since the seventies to find the right opportunity. When Mrs. Thomas had called him from Toronto to tell him her and her husband would be in Vancouver he couldn't pass up the chance.

His career would be over, but what the hell. Maybe he'd become a fry cook at some greasy spoon, or maybe a pool hustler after all. He was pretty good with the stick.

The restaurant manager. Now there was a sleazy piece of work.

A good frame up candidate. But the slime balls criminal record went back twenty years, and mostly for petty crimes, not anything with violence. Who would believe he'd graduated to murder after all this time.

Hard to believe the guy wanted to be a writer, which explained his meeting with the agent at the same hotel as Jack was staying.

And the dishwasher. He had served time for drug dealing. Small time stuff mostly.

Naw, the small town cop, the captain really loved that one.

Ben had made his captain an easy believer based on that fact. It was the case closer if there ever was one.

A thought suddenly occurred to him. Maybe the fat broad killed Kelly. He started to chuckle at his own joke.

Jessie stopped licking herself to stare up at him probably wondering what was so funny.

He shook his head. Naw, the poet was too esoteric to kill anyone.

12

Rose closed her notebook after she drew a straight blue line through the last item on her list.

She smiled to herself. Done. Ten years of planning were complete.

Jack would never suspect. And besides he was too stupid to realize how she'd done it.

Ben would make sure he made it home and all once more would be right with the world. More importantly the rules were meant to be obeyed.

If only Jack hadn't made that call like she knew he would, (he was so predictable). Maybe then none of this would've happened, and the little scheming bitch would still be alive.

The note she'd left for Jack to find had been a clue of inspired genius. Damn that Ben Harris is a clever man.

Kelly herself was no dummy, but not as clever as her. Rose kept to her rules. Consequently Cape Disappointment had claimed another victim.

The heavily loaded 747 shook as it lumbered down the runway then into the winter sky to take her home and away from her disappointment.

No man would break the rules on her watch ever again.

The Watcher of Wayburn Street

I TOOK A SIP OF THE HOT COFFEE and winced when it burned against my tongue. I should have waited for it cool down.

I look out the large picture window to see a man wearing a soiled powder blue track suit, his hair the color of steel wool, pushing a rusted grocery cart brimming with dumpster treasurers in the crosswalk on Wayburn Street.

I see the usual drug dealers on the other side of the street peddling their wares outside the abandoned fruit and vegetable store. In the dirty window of delicatessen next door one end of the GOING OUT OF BUSINESS sign hangs limp as it has for over a year.

I watched as cars, trucks and buses from the suburbs whizzed past another grizzled street veteran sitting hunchback-like on the cracked sidewalk, until the traffic light over the intersection warns them to stop. It changes to yellow, followed a few seconds later, to red.

Airbrakes sigh and brakes squeal as the hurried occupants of the assorted vehicles applied brakes and traffic comes to a stop. I watched the light over Wayburn change to green then northbound trucks; cars and buses leap forward like an unleashed dog to stream away.

This flotsam of traffic will continue all day, just as it has every day for the past eighteen years.

"Hi, Mr. Kenniphaas."

I look up to find Autumn Siu standing over me smiling warmly. She's a college student who works as a part time barista. Her dark eyes gaze at me and she seems pleased as usual to see me. Autumn, no more than twenty years old, her shoulder length rich black hair tied behind her oval shaped head into a pony tail, is busy clearing tables.

When she started working at Coffee Planet she made a point to learn the names of the regulars. Unlike me, Autumn is destined to go far in life with that attitude.

"Good morning, Autumn." I smiled as I rested my gnarled hands on the end of the brass handle of my cane.

"See anything interesting today?"

I chuckled drily. "No, not today." I lowered my voice. "But you should have seen yesterday." I wiggled my bushy white eyebrows comically.

Her laugh was like a wind chime. "Oh, Mr. Kenniphaas, you are so silly." With another laugh she walked away pushing a cart with a plastic dish tub on top. I watched her busily plucking empty coffee cups, plates covered in muffin crumbs and flakes of pastry, and crumpled napkins, off the round oak tables scattered through out the dimly lit coffee shop. The dishes rattled as the cart rolled over the brown-and-gray textured floor tiles.

"Cinnamon latté," Jessie Walker, a willowy blonde, called from behind the chest-high drink station where the specialty coffees were prepared.

Tamber Lickiss, heavy-set with shoulder-length hair the color of sun bleached seashells, dressed in tattered blue jeans and new white Nikes, waddled to the counter and snatched the paper cup with the Saturn-shaped logo on the side. The strong odor of cinnamon filled my senses from my seat on the other side of the shop.

I knew Tamber well. She had been my cleaning lady until three months ago when I caught her stealing. Tamber was a nice young woman, but lazy, and I suspect has a problem with alcohol, or perhaps something worse.

At first she denied lifting the money from my wallet until I showed her the bank slip with the sixty dollars I'd withdrawn that morning. When confronted with the fact my wallet now contained only forty dollars she admitted her guilt.

I felt pity for her and told her I wouldn't involve the police and said she was to keep the twenty dollars as severance pay. Involving the police would involve the outside world. I preferred to handle such matters privately.

She seemed grateful, but two weeks later she badmouthed me in front of her friends when we encountered each other at Planet Coffee. Her language revealed a solid understanding of street life, but her grammar was atrocious and her reference to me as a lover of swine was puzzling. She even threatened me with bodily harm, as if I had done something awful to her.

At first I was annoyed she would embarrass me at my coffee shop, but I let it go. No confrontation is worth it. I forgave her.

I watched Tamber take the cup, and heard her too-many-cigarettes-damaged voice complain about the lack of foam on the coffee.

After Jessie explained the amount of foam was standard, Tamber grunted, then begrudgingly walked away and headed for the door leading to the small parking lot next to the shop. Her sea-green eyes narrowed to slits as she scuffed past me. The tinny bell above the door rang brightly when it closed behind her.

I was surprised when my shoulders relaxed now that she was gone. Was I really afraid of her? I shrugged and went back to watching the bank located diagonally across the street from the coffee shop.

Autumn had indeed missed the excitement yesterday. I didn't tell her about it because she might worry and what good would that do?

###

Yesterday, fifteen minutes after I'd sat at my usual table, a large black car with spinning chrome wheels and tinted windows pulled up in front of the bank. Three men exited the still running car with balaclavas covering their faces. They were dressed head-to-toe in black and they each carried a pistol in one hand, and a pillowcase in the other.

I recall thinking it odd one of the pillowcases had a flowery pattern.

The men entered the bank.

The robbers were back in a few minutes, the pillowcases bulging, and quickly disappeared into the car.

Planet Coffee's windows shimmered when the car's powerful engine roared and then it sped away with a squeal of tires, leaving behind a cloud of blue smoke.

Within seconds I heard the wail of sirens headed this way. A plethora of police cars soon arrived to close the intersection.

It was then I spotted Tamber appear from the alley behind the bank. She was talking on her cell phone and a wide grin split her freckled features.

Even though I couldn't hear what she was saying there was something in the way she talked that made me curious. She seemed excited and her eyes scanned the growing throng of the curious, and the cops in their navy blue uniforms, as if she were enjoying the mayhem caused by the bank robbery.

Lastly, an unmarked car, with a red flashing light on its slate-gray roof, stopped in front of the bank entrance. A tall white-haired man exited the passenger side, while a younger blonde woman, her eyes hidden by dark sunglasses, exited the driver's side. They both wore navy blue suits and white shirts neither wore a tie.

I could see the bulge in their jackets made by a gun on their hips. When a breeze briefly caused their jackets to billow open I saw a flash of sunlight off the gold badges on their belts.

The two detectives went to the sidewalk and began a conversation with a statesman-like uniformed policeman holding a portable radio in his left hand. There were gold bars on the collar of his uniform shirt. They spoke for several minutes then the woman swiveled her head to face the coffee shop. She turned back to the two men then nodded and headed for the crosswalk.

She was coming here to interview witnesses. I considering leaving before she arrived, then immediately dismissed the idea when she broke into a trot, and I saw two uniformed behemoths had moved to guard the coffee shop's only door.

My hands trembled. No one was leaving, including me.

###

Her name was Emily Harris, Detective, Third Grade. Her tone was surprisingly gentle as I listened and watched her question each person in the shop until she got to me.

My table faced the bank. I was the best witness. I was the one she really wanted to interview.

I noticed her eyes flit to me several times during her interviews with the others. I felt a single bead of perspiration run down the side of my face. I was afraid to wipe it away.

But I realized she'd made a mistake. She questioned everyone together rather than separately. I'd watched enough cop shows to know the procedures. Divide and conquer was standard police practice.

What I failed to consider was no one here was involved in the robbery. We weren't suspects we were witnesses.

Once it was my turn I discovered Emily's intelligent hazel eyes were kind and her voice was dry and she was a good listener.

I told her everything I'd seen describing the car, the robbers, and pillowcases. Her brow wrinkled slightly as I told her about the pattern on one of the pillowcases.

"That's important isn't it?" I'd provided what I considered a salient fact.

Emily shrugged her right shoulder. "Hard to say. Could be."

To say I was disappointed falls far short of how I deflated I felt at that moment.

Sensing my disappointment she changed subjects. "What do you do?"

Emily (she encouraged me to call her Emily) fingered the page of the notebook open on the table in front of as her curious eyes studied me. A black pen lay on the table next to the book. After she'd recorded my name, address, and other tombstone data, she'd put the pen down and crossed her legs.

"I used to teach high school English."

Her eyes widened. "Really? How long ago?"

"Eighteen years."

The corners of her mouth curled. "That long, huh?" I nodded. She swiveled her head to look at her fellow cops setting up a band of banana-yellow tape to bar the unwanted from entering the bank then she looked back at me. "What do you do now?"

Without pausing to consider my words I responded. "I watch."

Her eyebrows arched. "Really?" She nodded toward the parking lot to my left on the other side of the window. "Out there?"

"Yes. Huh...I mean the world..." I shrugged and forced my mouth to form a grin. "I mean not the whole world just Wayburn Street."

She smiled. "You're the watcher of Wayburn Street, huh?"

"I guess that'd be the best way to describe me."

Emily uncrossed her legs and shifted forward on the wooden chair. "So tell me, who did you see doing something unusual at the time of the robbery?"

I wondered how she knew. "Huh, there's this woman..."

"A woman?" Her brow creased.

"Huh, yes. Tamber Lickiss. She was talking on her cell phone right after the robbery."

Emily sat back in her chair and frowned. "And why is this important?"

I realized I was going to sound silly. "Tamber was talking funny." She raised one eyebrow. "I mean, she was laughing and joking."

"People laugh and joke on cell phones every day. What makes this different?"

I hesitated. <u>Do I tell her</u>? "Tamber stole money from me," I explained at last.

After a few more questions about Tamber, and where she lived, Emily thanked me and I headed home secure in the knowledge I'd done the right thing.

Today, though, Tamber made me nervous. Why should I be nervous? It's not like I knew for sure she had anything to do with the bank robbery.

I was lost in my own world when a voice jolted me back to reality. "Mr. Kenniphaas?"

I looked up and it was Autumn again, this time with a steaming mug of coffee in one hand. "I noticed your coffee was cold and thought you'd want a fresh one."

I smiled and glanced down at the half empty mug in front of me. Just as she said it was cold and thoroughly unappealing. I looked back at her. "Thank you, Autumn. You are a dear."

She smiled, set the mug on the table, and picked up the old one. I reached for my wallet.

Autumn held up one hand. "No charge, Mr. Kenniphaas."

I smiled at her. "Thank you again."

"No worries," Autumn said with a giggle as she spun round and disappeared in the direction of the washrooms. I glanced at my watch. 11:30. Washroom inspection time. I smiled to myself. The girl was certainly conscientious. Like I said she's destined to go far.

I started when the door to the parking lot burst inward to bang hard against the condiment stand.

A knot formed in my stomach as I watched Tamber Lickiss enter, her features twisted in a sneer, her eyes filled with an unearthly rage. She was breathing hard and the fingers of her right hand gripped a large hunting knife.

She went directly to the counter. "Give me the money," she growled at Jerry Smalls who stood behind the counter. She held up the knife to emphasize her demand.

There were two other people besides me in the coffee shop. Helen Madras, in her blue dental assistant's uniform, and a young man I didn't recognize with a goatee and long auburn hair that drooped across his shoulders. They were both frozen apparently unable to move.

Jerry's features were ashen and his hands trembled as he fumbled with the cash register's buttons trying to open it.

"Hurry it up or your dead," threatened Tamber wielding the knife at poor frightened Jerry.

Finally, Jerry managed to open the drawer. "Step back," commanded Tamber. He did. She rose on the toes of her sneakers and peered into the tray. She snorted her disgust. "That's it? It isn't enough to buy cat food."

Spinning around her hard eyes traveled over Helen and the longhaired boy. "Give 'em your wallets," she grunted.

This made Helen and the boy finally move. They had their wallets on the table within seconds.

Tamber snatched Helen's wallet from the table.

Still holding the knife in one hand she opened Helen's wallet and a twisted smiled crossed her features. "Now this is more like it." She pulled out five one hundred dollar bills stuffed them in the pocket of her jeans then let Helen's wallet drop to the floor with a smack.

"That's rent money," Helen whispered.

Tamber glared at her. "Keep talkin', lady, and you won't have to worry about rent.

Helen averted her eyes as her shoulders slumped and she began to sob.

"Hey! What's going on?" Autumn?

Tamber swung round the knife held waist high. The tip of the blade made contact with Autumn's shirt and tore a rip across her belly.

I don't remember much of what happened next. I do have a foggy memory of a sickening odor of cigarettes and stale beer.

They tell me I lost it. Apparently I shouted Autumn's name as I struck Tamber's hand with the handle of my cane and managed to knock the knife free. It fell to the floor with a clatter. I'm told I broke her wrist.

I felt bad about hurting her.

The kid with the goatee and the long hair turned out to be an uncover cop who arrested Tamber.

The next thing I recall was sitting at my usual table at Coffee Planet across from a smiling Detective Emily Harris.

"You okay?"

"Yes, I think so, Emily." I blinked away the fog clouding my brain. "What happened?"

"We got the bank robbers." I nodded. "And as you suspected Tamber was involved. She was the lookout."

"Oh. Really?" I narrowed my eyes. "What's going to happen to her?"

Emily's pencil thin eyebrows rose. "She's been charged as an accomplice in the bank robbery, and with the attempted armed robbery of this coffee shop." She shrugged. "I expect she's going to be going away for a long time."

I looked around and realized Helen, Jerry, Autumn, and the long haired kid were gone. "Where is everyone?"

"They finished their statements so I had a constable drive them home."

My heart rate increased. "Then Autumn's ok?"

Emily's mouth curled at the corners as before. "She's fine, but she'll have to buy another shirt." I nodded as the tension in my shoulders eased and my heart rate returned to normal. She added, "You're quite the hero ya know?"

I shook my head. "No. Not me. I watch. I don't get involved."

Emily reached out to pat the back of my hand and chuckled. "No, sorry, Mr. Kenniphaas, you're now officially the hero of Wayburn Street."

I knew she was right. The world had changed.

"You want me to add a charge of robbery for the money she stole from you?"

I looked into her hazel eyes and saw she was serious. "No, of course not."

She frowned. "Why not?"

"I already forgave her for that."

One eyebrow shot up on Emily's forehead. "And what about today? Are you going to forgive her for today?"

"Yes, of course. And I'll visit her in jail. She needs help."

Emily shook her head and stood. "Okay, Mr. Kenniphaas. I'll give you a ride home."

We walked outside into the small parking lot to be greeted by a light rain. For the first time I noticed my clothes reeked of stale coffee.

I spend far too much time in this coffee shop hiding from life.

The buzz of traffic on Wayburn Street filled my senses as Emily opened the passenger side door of the unmarked police car.

"Tamber said she was going to hurt you," said Emily as I sank into the passenger seat of the large sedan.

Before I could respond she closed the car door and walked around the hood of the car. I adjusted my weight as I sank into the plush cloth seat, sighed, and shut my eyes.

I smiled to myself. Emily's right, the watcher of Wayburn Street is officially retired. And I wasn't afraid of Tamber or anyone else.

I had become the hero of my own story. I wasn't going to stand by and just watch anymore. It was time to change the world.

A Day Without Sunshine

IT SEEMS EVERY TIME I SMELL BLOOD it's a good day.

The iron smell of the dark ruby liquid means I'm going to pay my rent, and maybe even eat. For sure my bartender is happy because I'll settle my tab. As it turned out however this blood was the start of the worst day of my life.

Today I found her body in a pool of blood in the hallway outside my dingy office door. Since I hadn't had my morning coffee her death gave me a sour stomach. And I hate a sour stomach.

Hell of a day to quit smoking. Before I quit the weed the first cigarette of the day masked the smells of the putrid mornings in my world. But not today.

In my line of work a dead mystery woman is just another day at the office except this was a rich broad.

You know the type, a gal from the right side of the tracks who lives to visit the wrong side for the excitement.

I was born, live, and have always worked, on the wrong side of the tracks so I fully expect to die on the wrong side. The hourglass-shaped, copper-haired woman that lay dead on my doorstep had beat me to the other side.

Problem was a woman dressed in an Anna Sui Organza cocktail dress in this part of town was a like a neon sign that reads FREE SAMPLES. (Good thing every gray organza cocktail dress, with a black tulle layer and sequin embroidery, has a label under the neck line just like any off-the-shelf-Wal-Mart knockoff)

In the circumstances it wasn't a surprise she was murdered--and had her no doubt matching handbag stolen--but why did she have to die on my doorstep, with my business card gripped in the pale lifeless fingers of her left hand? She'd found her excitement but now I was somehow involved, and I didn't know why. I really hate it when I don't know why. Guess that's why I became a PI.

After I'd made the call to my homicide contact, Inspector Lyle Crowder, to notify him of the untimely death, I stood over the corpse in order to study her closely.

Her natural red hair looked freshly permed, and her cinnamon tinged perfume masked the usual door of urine and decay prevalent in the three story brick walk up I call my home away from home. Though my definition of home is fluid.

The twenty-year old overstuffed couch in my two-room rented office had depressions that matched my lean frame. I'd only been sleeping on it for the past nine months and already it fit like a glove.

High cheekbones and lightly applied makeup made her beautiful in my eyes. Slightly muscular calves accentuated her legs—long and shapely—. She obviously worked out, but not so much as to become the female version of Governor Arnie. I think the exercise gurus call it body sculpting. Her appearance suggested she had a personal trainer. I have a personal trainer too. My bartender, Mickey Risk, ensures I bend my elbow on a daily basis.

Crowder appeared in the hallway accompanied by his partner Wally Esper. I don't care much for Wally. His appearance reminds of a weasel, with a personality and attitude to match. It was the same in every town I drifted into. The good homicide dicks always seemed to have weasels for partners. And I loathe every one of 'em.

Wally's beady eyes narrowed as he realized it was me who'd called them out so early in the a.m. I nodded to the two cops as they came up to stand beside me over the redhead's lifeless corpse.

Crowder looked painfully thin in his baggy standard cop issue cheap dark blue suit, white shirt, and narrow black tie. His baldhead was covered by an ink-black fedora. I'm glad hats for men have made a comeback. Sam Spade would be proud.

Not that I was much better in my only five-year-old pinstriped navy suit that had seen better days. My thin dark tie was loose at the unbuttoned collar of my one clean white shirt. I may only have one suit and tie but at least I own four white shirts. Like Lyle I usually wear my fedora when I go out. Sure, it's chocolate brown, and clashes with my suit, but then I'm no slave to fashion.

I smelled the cigarette Lyle had just finished—I felt a twinge of envy. The tobacco smoke mingled with Wally's drug store aftershave. The weasel didn't have to get all dolled up just for little 'ol me.

"Hey, Stiletto," said Lyle, in his patented bored style meant to disarm the suspect.

Naturally I expected to be considered a suspect. After all an ex-cop who'd made some mistakes on the job was the perfect patsy.

But I also knew Lyle would find any excuse to eliminate me from his mental checklist. He knew I wasn't the cold-blooded killer type.

Sure I'm a screw up, but I'd certainly never murder anyone. He also knew I had a nose for the less than obvious clues that have so often resulted in the bad guy riding old sparky into the next world. And Lyle lived for convictions. Besides I'd rather love 'em than kill 'em, especially with a looker like the dead redhead sprawled across the scarred wooden floor boards.

All I needed to do was help him to eliminate me from his usual suspects list. "Hey, Crowder...Esper," I added, nodding to Wally who grimaced as he stuffed his hands in the pockets of his cheap brown suit pants and rocked back slightly on his heels.

"Had your coffee yet?" asked Crowder as his analytical blue eyes scanned the redhead's body.

"Nope."

Crowder nodded. "Too bad. Me neither."

"Don't you ever shave?" Lyle quipped eyeing my four days growth of beard.

"Once a week, whether I need to or not," I said.

Lyle chuckled then sank to his haunches and peered hard at my business card held in her fingers. He grunted. "Looks like a plant to me."

Esper snorted and opened his mouth to speak. Lyle shot him a look. Wally's wide mouth snapped shut and he appeared properly cowed. I wanted to smile at the weasels discomfort but held back.

"Throat cut. Too bad." He shook his head. "Rich dame," added Lyle before rising to stand and stuffed his hands in his pants pockets. He'd drawn the same conclusion I had from her makeup and clothes. He glanced at me. "Any handbag?" I shook my head.

"Uh, uh…" A frown creased his forehead. "Know her?"

"Never saw her before I stepped outta my office door this morning—"

"Did you hear sumthing…kinda early…" He was right. It was only five in the a.m.

I shook my head. "Nope. I was going to the corner, to that twenty-four/seven coffee shop…"

"Huh, huh…" He tipped his hat back slightly on his head with his right index finger. "Wally, when are the crime scene boys gonna be here?" he said, not taking eyes off the victim.

Wally's eyes shifted to me then back to his boss. "Uhhh…I don't know…"

"Find out," said Crowder. "Go down to the street and show 'em the way up here."

"But it's raining," whined the weasel.

Crowder cast his cool gaze over Wally who nodded sheepishly then, without another word, walked away down the hall to the stairs. His heavy footsteps echoed on the squeaky wooden planks until they faded as he disappeared down the stairs. My shabby office was on the third floor.

Now that we were alone, Lyle's shoulders relaxed and he looked at me, his blue eyes steady with an edge of the curious common to most detectives.

"You piss someone off lately?" he said, his tone suggested more of a statement than a question.

I shrugged my shoulders. Truth was I was always pissing someone off. The job description of a private dick includes an innate ability to piss people off at least once a week without getting killed. Problem was this was a rich broad, and if someone with bucks to burn wanted me dead they could have hired a pro and taken me out five minutes after the check cleared.

"The usual suspects; drug dealers, cheating husbands, pimps, and other assorted bottom feeders not worth mentioning." I shook my head. "No one in her league, that's for sure."

Lyle frowned. He stepped toward me and placed one hand on my left shoulder.

"Listen, Jazz, I know you only been in town for nine months, and we don't know each other too well, but if there's something you're not telling me..." He let his words hang for several seconds his sympathetic eyes locked on mine then he added, "I'd hate to see you murdered too."

A lightning bolt of realization struck me. "Who's dead?" I asked slowly.

Lyle dropped his hands to his side and he leaned against the hallway wall compressing the peeling yellowed wallpaper with his bulky frame. His eyes dropped to the floor his chin on his chest.

"We found Bobbi Diamond last night," he said, his baritone voice just above a whisper. Lyle slashed his index finger across his throat to demonstrate Bobbi had been killed in the same fashion as our mystery woman.

I knew Diamond. She was a rival PI who had an office over on Carpenter Park Drive. She had four PI's under contract working for her. Too often I'd thought about applying to be one of them, but my gut was telling me I was gone, gone, gone---and soon. I had never made it a year in one place before I got the itch to get outta Dodge.

Diamond's crew took on cases so far out of my league they might as well be on another planet.

Her cases usually involved the elite movers and shakers of the city. The papers were chock full of divorce hurricanes between the rich and powerful, and Diamond's PI agency was usually at the eye of those storms.

"Cap's on my ass to snag Diamond's killer."

I smirked. "Yeah, I know."

Everyone on the street knew Diamond had done the chief of the PD a favor. Her operatives had delivered naughty pics of the chief's wife and a city councilman doing the nasty. Rumor was the chief pulled some strings, and the judge who granted him the divorce had sealed the court records never to be make their way to public eyes.

Unfortunately, some of the more revealing pictures—with black lines over the naughty bits—were splashed across the morning paper two days ago. The editor claimed a courier delivered the pictures, and he claimed the return address was an empty lot.

"Let's get that coffee," I suggested. Crowder heaved a heavy sigh and nodded. I liked this guy. I wanted to help him.

***

We were seated at one of three dark stained wooden tables, dotted with mug rings, each with a steaming cup of mountain grown goodness in front of us. Another thing Lyle and I had in common we both drank our coffee black.

I closed my eyes and took a sip of the hot brew. The aromatic earthiness of the fresh roasted beans cleared my senses of death. I made a yummy sound and smirked. I opened my eyes to see Lyle's attention was on the street.

I almost spewed the coffee across the table. He was looking in the direction of a white limousine that had stopped in front of my building. Since when did limousines stop in front of my building? This didn't look good even to me, and I knew I'd done nothing wrong.

The driver, a giant of a black man dressed in an ink-black chauffeur's uniform complete with the cap and white shirt and matching tie, was right out Driving Miss Daisy. Except this guy was no Morgan Freeman. He had a bull neck and a forehead that hung low over coal hard eyes. From his left ear, at the end of a gold chain, dangled a brilliant diamond that would have made Liz Taylor envious. His suit jacket bulged from the rippling muscles barely contain by the expensive fabric.

It seemed body guard/chauffeur work paid better than licensed private detective.

Maybe I should…naw, I enjoy my freedom too much.

"Looks like you got visitors," said Lyle, his eyes focused on the long white car that seemed to cover the half block. My building sat in the middle of the block. Lyle turned his cool gaze on me; his blue eyes were like twin lamps the old-time movie cops used to interrogate suspects.

I looked away from Lyle's quizzical eyes in time to see the driver walk up to weasel-boy Wally. Watching the big man tower over the cheap detective I felt a pleasant sensation. Wally looked scared of the big guy. Good for you, bodyguard guy.

The passenger was obviously going to wait curbside in the comfort of the luxury box on wheels while the driver fetched me. How did I know it was me they were looking for you ask? Given a choice of occupants of a dilapidated building that included an importer of dime store trinkets, assorted crack dealers, and one slightly rumpled private dick, who else could it be? Especially with one of their own kind found dead outside my office.

When I looked back Lyle had dropped his gaze to the mug of steaming coffee in front of him.

"I think you better go talk to them. I suspect they won't be too eager to talk to me."

"Yeah," I agreed. I got up from the table and started for the door.

"Oh, and Jazz…" I stopped and swiveled my eyes to his, which had fixed themselves on me. "Anything you find out…?" He didn't need to finish the sentence. He had cut me some slack to get to the bottom of this mess. After all, the dead girl had my business card in her fingers when she was found and now someone who probably loved her had shown up.

Sure, Lyle could have run us all in and held everyone until someone talked, but he knew I'd get to the bottom of the case faster if I was out. After all I had done it before. And he knew I'd share anything I found out with him. He knows I'm reliable. Lyle is a good cop with unparalleled instincts for people. I nodded and exited the coffee shop.

I walked toward the limo with its dark shaded windows and felt unseen eyes study me. The bodyguard who had been cowing Wally turned to look at me. His dark emotionless eyes narrowed slightly. He ignored Wally and moved to stand on guard beside the long car his hands folded in front of him.

As I approached the passenger door the window slid down with a soft burr.

The car's seats were covered in wine-red leather. Once beside the car I discovered the passenger was a woman dressed in black, a pale complexion, and brilliant blue eyes. She studied me up and down as I stared open mouthed at her. High cheekbones and long chestnut brown hair famed a face that only God could have made. The neckline of her dress ended at the base of her long tapered neck, and the slight swell of her bosom was covered a strand of ivory white pearls each flawless and exactly the same size and shape. Her matching pearl earrings adorned her perfectly shaped ear lobes. She would be the ideal model for the Venus Di Milo.

"Mr. Stiletto?" she said softly. Her voice reminded me of the sound of a summer breeze, with an edge of huskiness that would wake a dead man. I felt a stir in my loins but forced the dirty thoughts away by clearing my throat.

"Ahem…yes, I'm Stiletto…Jazz Stiletto…"

"I understand my sister was found dead outside your office this morning."

***

After the ride in Ms. Penny-Anne Robespierre's—of the Rhode Island Robespierre's—stretch limousine I felt somewhat revived.

The form fitted seat that encased my weary body like a cocoon, combined with the strong coffee, had managed to revive me for what was sure to be a fun filled day. That is if your definition of fun includes murder, secrets, and lies.

Rich people and their games. These people have too much time on their hands.

The car finally stopped outside a mansion right out of Gone With the Wind complete with four roman columns that stood guard on either side of an entryway large enough to shove a grand piano through. The twin doors leading to the interior of the massive structure— that towered some thirty feet over my head—were massive constructs made of what appeared to be heavy gage steel. From my days in the army I recognized the windows were the type designed to stop every type of munitions short of a howitzer, and even that would have to be fired at close range. The house was a fortress.

And the surrounding grounds were bursting with colorful flowerbeds with red, purple, yellow, and pink. Chrysanthemum's, begonia, black-eyed Susan's and Jacob's ladder were everywhere. Someone had a green thumb. Given the bucks these people had they likely had a gardener or two or three on the payroll.

The twin doors swung open as the car came to a stop and the black Mr. Clean hopped out—he moved faster than I would have thought him capable given his mass—and held the passenger door open. Ms. Robespierre stepped out with the chauffeur holding one of her hands in his meaty paw. I shuffled across the long leather bench seat and stepped out. The chauffer—who's name was Butch—didn't offer me his hand in fact he glared at me.

"Love you too," I whispered just loud enough for the behemoth to hear me. I could see the burst of anger in his eyes and the muscles of his massive arms rippled beneath his suit as he restrained himself from tearing me in half like he no doubt did to the Yellow Pages. This visit with the rich and infamous had the potential to be a lot of fun.

I followed Ms. Robespierre to the door where a real tuxedoed butler stood beside the entryway. Of course, he looked more like a mob enforcer in a monkey suit than an English butler. He was the white version of Butch the bodyguard. I wondered if he made more on this gig than as a WWE wrestler. He certainly had the build for that line of work. Difference was the average WWE wrestler didn't have the bulge of a cannon in a shoulder holster beneath his suit jacket.

What was it with these people? Had a war broken out I hadn't heard about?

"Thank you, Hugo," said Ms. Robespierre, with a slight nod of her head as we entered and the butler closed and bolted the steel doors with the clang of steel on steel. Oh goody, Fortress Robespierre.

"Follow me to the library," ordered Ms. Robespierre. I followed her dutifully with a shrug. If I hadn't I was pretty sure I would have quickly become lost. There were four sets of heavy twin oak doors that led off the foyer and a massive spiral staircase that led to the upper floors. The floor was gray and white speckled marble and there was a large crystal chandelier that hung from the ceiling, which was at least twenty feet high. Man, I'd hate to have to pay the heat and light bills for this castle.

Ms. Robespierre chose what was behind twin doors number four to our left. We entered a room lined with oak shelves that ran from waist high to the ceiling and covered every wall.

A woman, with an angry jagged scar across her left cheek, dressed in a white maid's uniform, poured what smelled like orange pekoe tea into fine white china cups from a solid silver tea pot set on a silver tray that rested on a round solid oak table.

The table was book ended by matching burgundy leather Canterbury wing chairs. Next to each chair was floor a lamp. The cone-shaped hood directed the light from the bulb onto the person seated in the chair. Imagine, a library were someone actually read a book? What will they think of next?

Ms. Robespierre indicated, with a sweep of her left hand, I should sit. Like the good little PI I am I sat.

The maid, with one blue and one green eye, dirty brown hair, a pale complexion, and a slight paunch around her middle appeared to be in her mid-forties, handed me one the cups of tea on a saucer. I nodded and smiled thinly at her but her expression was blank as if she didn't see me. She turned and did likewise to Ms. Robespierre then left the room closing the door behind her with a soft thud.

"How well did you know Sunshine, Mr. Stiletto?" said Ms. Robespierre before she took a tentative nip at the hot tea.

"Your sister's name is Sunshine?" I said.

"I take it you didn't know her then?"

I shook my head and took a sip of the tea. I felt the hot bitter liquid burn as it hit my taste buds then traveled down my throat.

A door hidden behind a wall of books opened and a man dressed in a black sweatshirt, black jean, and black Nike's appeared. He had wiry dirty blonde hair cut into a flat top and piercing blue eyes. His face was hairless, smooth and tanned. Given his medium build and wiry physique I suspected he jogged. In my world we call joggers people who run for their lives, in this world that's how they stay in shape. It was hard to imagine running for fun in my world of unpaid bookies and assorted street toughs.

"I'll make him talk, Penny!" The unidentified man lunged across the room at me. With the flick of my wrist I splashed hot tea across his square jawed mug. He howled, his hands covered his face and he stumbled backward until he fell against a wall of books.

"Was that really necessary?" said Ms. Robespierre dryly. "Nathan only wanted to talk."

"When a man comes at me with blood in his eye I usually react poorly, self preservation being what it is," I said, with a faint smile on my lips. "May I call you Penny?"

Nathan had slid to the carpeted floor whimpering like a wounded puppy his hands still held over his reddened features.

Penny Robespierre ignored my suggestion of familiarity.

"I'd like to introduce you to Nathan Barber, my fiancé. Please excuse his rash behavior; he tends to be wound a little too tight for his own good."

I smiled. "Well now, that's very different. When's the happy day?"

"It was to be this Saturday but now I'm not so sure." Her gaze drifted over her fiancée like she was examining the on-sale ground chuck at the supermarket. "Now that's Sunshine's dead I'm not sure there's any need at all."

"But darling," said a suddenly alert Nathan, who'd risen to his feet and made his way to stand beside his betrothed's right side. "I love you and I want to be married—"

"To my money," Penny Robespierre finished for him sarcastically.

Nathan was either an Academy Award winning actor, or the most persuasive liar on the planet, evidenced by the look of abject horror on his second degree burned face. He certainly made me a believer.

"I'm afraid I don't understand…" I said.

Penny Robespierre turned slightly in her chair, the polished leather squeaked softly, and I detected the scent of her cinnamon tinged perfume over the odor of her over heated fiancé.

"When our father died seven years ago he made a stipulation in his will that if the two of us survived the first one to marry would inherit the bulk of his estate...."

"And the other?"

Penny shrugged and suddenly avoided eye contact, the powerful woman once more a little girl. "She would get a trust of two million dollars with which to live a comfortable life, wanting for nothing, and the use of the guest house on the property."

"So I gather the estate is large..."

"Forty-seven billion."

"Huh, uhhh...I see..." Of course what I saw was a clear motive for murder. Now I knew why she wanted to hire a low rent dick like yours truly. And it explained Fort Apache. But...

"What if one of you died...prematurely or, to be blunt, what if one of you had an unexplained accident?"

"If one of us aided in the demise of the other then the will would be null and void and the survivor would get nothing." She looked up into my eyes and hers narrowed. "I don't know about you, Mr. Stiletto, but once you've had the taste of a jewel encrusted spoon you're unwilling to settle for stainless steel."

"Yes, I can see that," I said.

Since my cutlery was usually of the plastic take out variety stainless steel was a luxury item to me.

"Well, then I gather you want me to find out who killed your sister...the question is why?"

Her perfectly plucked eyebrows rose in surprise on her baby-bottom smooth forehead. "Haven't you heard of sisterly love, Mr. Stiletto?"

Nathan, who had been silent to this point, snorted loudly.

Penny turned her head sharply and glared at her paramour. If it were possible I swear his face actually became redder and his eyes dropped to the floor to avoid the bullets that streamed from her eyes at him.

I sighed. I did need the money. I was planning to blow this town soon and why not use rich people's greenbacks to fund my ride? "OK, Ms. Robespierre. I get five hundred a day, plus expenses. I need the first five hundred now--in cash. I also require a list of places your sister might have been in the last forty eight hours, and a list of names, telephone numbers, and addresses of known associates and friends."

I shifted my body weight forward in the chair until my cheeks were near the edge then leaned toward her. "I was wondering...did Sunshine have a fiancée?" My gaze traveled upward to the cowardly Nathan. "Ya know, like 'ol Nate here."

"Not that I know of," Ms. Robespierre said bluntly. "My sister enjoys...enjoyed partying. She had many lovers. I hate to speak ill of the dead but... Sunshine was a slut. What man of quality and breeding would want a harlot and a drunk for a wife?"

"Yes," I agreed with a nod. "What man indeed?" I saw Nathan's robust features pale and his eyes go wide.

***

Half an hour later I was in a cab headed for my office. In my pocket were the five hundred, ten Benjamin's, and the two lists. One had the names of Sunshine Robespierre's usual haunts, the other was a list of names and addresses. It seemed little Sunshine had spread herself pretty thin. The list had fifty names. It would take me a month to track down everyone on the list. I needed help and I knew just who to call. My own personal cavalry, Lyle Crowder, and his sidekick Wally the weasel would be more than happy to shake these folks trees.

At least the list of hangouts was shorter, with five names. Two were nightclubs for the jet set crowd, while three were twenty-four hour restaurants, two of which were on the wrong side of the tracks. These names I planned to keep to myself—at least for now.

Before I went to my office, and called Crowder, I wanted to freshen up first.

I'd shower at the bar and put on a fresh shirt. I looked at my Timex. Mrs. Spitz should have returned my dry-cleaning to Mickey's bar by now. Mickey cut me a lot of slack given I was his best customer, and the fact that we had become friends.

As the cab turned onto my street I saw the flashing lights of an ambulance and several police cars. When we came to a stop outside Mickey's I spotted Crowder's unmarked forest green Chevy.

At the front entrance to the bar, the wood framed glass door was propped open, were two uniforms one male, one female. I paid the driver and walked toward to the female cop my eyes avoiding the male cop.

Her cool blue eyes watched me intently as I approached.

"Hello," I said as a small danced over my lips. "Is Detective Crowder around?"

"And who are you?" she said her voice deep and sexy.

"Stiletto. Jazz Stiletto."

Her eyes smiled. She nodded her head to indicate Lyle was inside Mickey's.

I reached inside to the inner pocket of my suit jacket and pulled out my wallet.

"You gonna bribe me?" she asked with an amused glance at her partner who smirked.

I handed her a business card from my wallet. Every time I arrive in a new city the first thing I do is get business cards.

I gave the female cop a wide toothy smile. "Of course not, officer. That would be illegal. No, I'd like you to take my card to Detective Crowder and tell him I'm out here. I'm certain he'd like to speak with me."

The female cop whose nametag read L Ribowitz frowned as she eyes scanned my card. "Phil, you stay here and keep an eye on this guy. I'll get the detective." Phil nodded his hands at his sides as if he were waiting for me to draw. Guy had seen too many westerns.

Two minutes later Lyle appeared with Wally in tow. He walked right up to me grabbed my left shoulder, spun me around, and pushed me hard into the wall next to the door. He then grabbed my left arm and bent it behind me. I felt the cold steel of handcuff being locked on my wrist. Next, with his full weight pressing me hard into the wall, he grabbed my other arm and snapped the cuff on my right wrist after twisting it behind my back. He gripped the collar of my suit jacket and pulled me backward. I felt the trickle of blood from one nostril and the taste of blood on my lower lip. I was stunned, helpless, and a prisoner.

"Jason Stiletto, I'm arresting you for the murders of Mickey Risk, Agnes Spitz, Sunshine Robespierre, and Bobbi Diamond. You have the right to--"

I didn't hear the rest of his legalese spiel; I knew it by rote anyway. My mind was spinning. How had this happened? I couldn't believe it; first Bobbi and Sunshine, now Mickey and Mrs. Spitz?

"Lyle! What the hell're you doin'? It's me... Jazz!"

Lyle finished reading me my rights and asked me if I understood them, particularly the part about keeping silent.

Wally eyed me evilly. The son of a bitch was enjoying this. I lunged at him and like the coward he was; he took a step backward and stumbled off the curb. The two uniforms exchanged knowing looks and shook their heads.

Lyle snorted in disgust and grabbed my left arm roughly and shoved me against his car. I felt like I'd been run into a brick wall. Black spots danced before my eyes. The cigarette smell coming from my former friend was stronger now that I was in his space.

He flung the passenger door of his unmarked car open, grabbed me again by my jacket collar, threw me bodily into the back seat and slammed the car door behind me.

I heard Lyle's muffled shout to Wally to get behind the wheel and drive. He was going to ride in the back with the prisoner—it took a moment for the fog that in my brain to clear before it registered Lyle meant me.

Lyle climbed in beside me and shoved me hard against the door handle; it dug hard into my side. I winced from the shot of pain that ran up my right side. "Do you have to be so rough?" I grumbled as I straighten to sit upright. Lyle said nothing, he kept his eyes focused forward his expression hard as granite.

"Where're we going?"

"The station."

I felt the car lurch beneath me and we began to move. The traffic was light and Wally quickly made his way to First and Albright. He stopped at a red light. I decided to try Lyle again.

"Lyle. I don't get it….why do you think I killed those people?"

His head turned slightly this time and one eye looked at me. His lips moved but no words came out. But that didn't matter. I knew what he'd wanted to say. He had just confirmed who was behind the murders. Lyle Crowder, my one remaining friend in the world, knew I was innocent.

When we arrived at the station Wally pulled into a parking spot far from the main entrance. The street lamp over this part of the lot had burned out so it was dark, and since the sky had decided to open up, rain peppered the Chevy's roof with a sound reminiscent of machine gun bullets. Boy, had my hitch in the army ever screwed up my imagination.

"Get lost, Wally." Esper opened the driver's door and quickly disappeared into the gloom.

Once we were alone with the rain and the stale air of cigarettes Lyle turned to look grim faced at me. The look behind his pained eyes told me the case of Sunshine Robespierre was at an end, or I was at an end. I also knew I had to fix this mess. Someone had to pay…for Mickey, for Mrs. Spitz…even for Sunshine. They had made this personal. Even if it meant my life I had to avenge them.

"I have to leave town," I said flatly.

Lyle nodded. "You OK? Sorry I was so rough. Had to make it look good. You gotta piece?"

I did. It was a Walther PPK, the James Bond gun. I kept it in an ankle holster. Won it in a poker game a few years back. I doubt the gangster I won it from bothered to register it, I know I certainly hadn't.

Funny thing was Lyle hadn't searched me when he arrested me.

Since that's standard police procedure it meant who ever had been watching didn't know police procedure. I replayed the image of the street outside Mickey's bar in mind. Yes. The white limo had been there. "Nope. Sorry, I don't carry."

Lyle looked disappointed. He shrugged and reached behind his suit jacket to the small of his back and pulled out a Smith and Wesson nine millimeter automatic. It was his back up piece. All cops carry a back up in case they get into a less than clean shoot or they need extra firepower. He handed me the gun. "Use this to hit me across the face." Lyle reached behind me and undid the handcuffs.

"I can't—"

"Do it or we're both dead." I nodded. I knew he was right. "I'll create a new name for you but you have to get out of town tonight. It has to look like you escaped."

"Why?"

"I have a family, Jazz…my son needs a father. But I also have a conscience. If you went to prison you'd have a shiv in you within the first week. You got too close, too fast. You were taken to the house to scope out how smart you were. Between us the frame job they tried at first didn't work so more murders with a hot tip to the chief's office did the trick.

The chief and the DA both have expensive tastes."

"Money and power?"

"Forty-Seven billion buys a lot insurance."

I nodded and studied the gun. I ran my index finger up the barrel and felt the roughness where the serial number had been filed off. Suddenly I lashed out and caught Lyle hard across the head. I heard a crack of bone and his outline fell forward onto the seat in from of me. I smelled blood. In the darkness I could hear him breathing.

Good. Now I had some unfinished business. Then would I leave town.

###

I placed Lyle's unconscious form against a chain link fence at the rear of the parking lot then drove away slowly so as not to arouse any suspicion.

I arrived at the chateau Robespierre just as the long white limousine pulled up to the front doors.

I watched as the hulking bodyguard opened the passenger door nearest the front doors. The butler stood with a silver tray upon which rested a single champagne glass. A victory drink no doubt.

I moved into position for a shot. The one thing they did well in the army was teach you how to shoot people. And I'd been good at it.

Now when you're going to kill someone, in fact three someone's you have to do it quickly. Unlike Hollywood where killers have these long expositions about the reasons and make the hero sweat it out before they do them, the reality is it takes about three seconds per shot. In a total of nine seconds I'd drilled three perfectly round holes dead center into three foreheads. The bullets ripped apart whatever intelligence these people had. They were no more.

***

I picked up my new identification papers from locker number seven at the bus station the next morning. I'd shaved and with five hundred dollars I'd bought a pair of blue jeans and a checkered work shirt and tanned work boots. I also had a duffle bag with an extra set of matching clothes and three pairs of underwear, socks and a shaving kit. The remainder of the money, three hundred and forty-seven dollars and twelve cents, paid for a bus ticket.

The two uniformed cops on the departure platform eyed me over closely. They checked my new driver's license, with the name Allan Harper, then let me board the Greyhound to my future.

The sky was overcast as the bus pulled away and joined traffic headed for the interstate. It started to rain by the time we merged with the traffic headed west.

An older man with steel gray hair who smelled of whiskey sat next to me. He offered me his flask, which I gladly accepted. I took a swig, the burning whiskey felt good, then handed the silver flask back to him.

In his gruff voice he said, "Looks like another day without sunshine."

"Yeah," I agreed, "another day without sunshine."

Dangerous Waters

I SHIVERED. Not because I just left the rain drenched, windswept Tradewinds Casino parking lot. And not because I suffered from the DT's, and really needed that first scotch Art the bartender had waiting for me in the Pacific Coast Bar on the second floor of the casino. It was because I almost tripped over the bloody corpse of Lincoln City's favorite used book dealer, Simon Yardley.

Simon lay at my feet in a puddle of water and blood, his throat marred by a nasty slash.

Simon's chocolate brown knit pants, and pale green shirt, were soaked through with water—salt water if my olfactory senses were still accurate.

"Freeze!" I froze, my heart racing.

I heard the familiar sound of a hammer being cocked on a revolver.

Back in the day I'd witnessed a lot of thirty-eight specials being fired at paper targets. And I knew all too well the damage hot lead could do to human flesh. Unfortunately, I also knew the casino security guards were older than dirt.

Old age, poor reflexes, and clouded minds, when paired with deadly force. It made me nervous.

As a writer I pride myself on knowing a lot of otherwise useless information. In this case I know too much.

"Hey, pops." I spoke slowly, and I hoped friendly, as I raised my hands over my head. "It's me Bert Sump." I glanced over my left shoulder and saw Parker Thomas, his gun gripped in both trembling hands. His gray-blue eyes flitted between me and poor Simon.

I closed my eyes and sighed.

Park is a fan. Since my fame from the bestseller days left the building with Elvis, having one loyal fan is a treasure more valuable than gold.

"I know, Mr. Simp, but don't move. The sheriff is on his way."

"Huh, Park, can I at least lower my arms?"

"Yeah, sure, Mr. Simp." With relief I let my arms drop to my sides. Physical exertion and I are old adversary's.

At three in the a.m., the sheriff, a new man I'd not met, was no doubt at home sawing down forests. Besides a December storm was in full swing outside. On a day like this a warm bed is man's best friend.

Winter storms and high winds make the ocean go mad at this time of year. Impassionate television news anchors, with perfect teeth and sculpted hair, love to tell tales of fierce waves pounding the shores of Lincoln City threatening to drag the summer-settlers way-too-expensive homes into the sea.

Local radio told of the powerful surf overpowering the breakwater at the Green Creek Bridge to sweep away a large section of highway. This cut Lincoln City in two.

I was grateful to be on the casino side of the highway, so I was nearer Art's bar.

And, according to the radio, the torrent coming from the boiling, ink-black clouds had washed out the highways both in and out of town. I considered trying to figure out how large a cubit is, but since I am a sinner by nature I decided against it. God doesn't want such as me in His heaven.

A distinctly feminine voice behind me startled me, "Hey, Parker." A draw of breath then she added, "Whoa, is that a dead body?"

"Hi, Deputy. Yes, and this is the killer."

Great, a woman deputy who thinks dead bodies are cool, and an old man who thinks I killed a book dealer. What possible motive could I have to murder Simon; he refuses to carry my third stink book because it's only good for lining the bottom of birdcages?

Of course, when I thought about it that's really not a bad motive.

"Deputy, do you mind if I stop being the model for the ice sculpture on the buffet so we can talk?"

"Sure."

I turned and met the pretty brunette's big brown eyes. She filled out her tan-colored sheriff department uniform like Pam Anderson filled out her bathing suit. Without thinking I blurted, "Hey, beautiful where you been all my life?"

The corners of her wide mouth curled slightly. "You're kidding, right?"

My cheeks grew warm. "Yeah, of course."

Her tanned brow wrinkled and one eyebrow arched. "Aren't you Max Acton?"

While I'm always pleased to be recognized but that name still makes me cringe. I made a mental note to send my former agent another hate e-mail for insisting on the inane pseudonym.

"My real name is Bert Simp."

The deputy crossed her arms over the swell of her bosom. "Hmmm, I think I like the fake name better."

Great, she thinks Max Acton is the better name. I suppressed the urge to groan. "Have we met?"

"Nope." Her eyes shifted to scan the dead body. "Isn't that Simon Yardley?"

"Yes," said Park who, much to my relief, had holstered his gun. "I think he's been murdered."

The deputy's eyes met mine and a brief smile passed over her lips. I shrugged. "Deputy Marne Locke." Her eyes stayed locked on mine while she tilted her head to indicate Simon. "You know him?"

"Certainly, he's a friend."

Marne nodded then her gaze shifted to Park. "What about you, Parker?"

Park shrugged his narrow shoulders while shifting his feet uneasily. His leather holster squeezed in time to his movements. New leather does tend to be noisy.

"How do you know Yardley?" I walked across the casino floor to liberate a chair from the row of chairs near the entrance doors. The chairs were padded and my butt was getting cold. It was like there was a draft coming from somewhere. Very odd for a casino to have drafts.

They like to make the guests—a very genteel term for sheep ripe for the fleecing—as comfortable as possible, at least until they've emptied their bank accounts into the slot machines, or added to the bankers stacks of chips at the craps table.

The lights flickered then dimmed. I looked up at the lights on the ceiling far above the casino floor. What's going on?

Marne must be a mind reader because she cleared up the mystery immediately. "I was upstairs in the office when I got the call."

"About Simon?"

"Ho, not that. The roads are washed out. The Sheriff is madder 'en a wet dog with fleas that he can't get here." She paused and crinkles appeared at the corners of her eyes telling me she didn't much care for the new sheriff. "No, I was already here meeting with the Casino's Chairman of the Board about a theft."

The lights flickered again. I thought they were going to go out all together. After a few seconds of uncertainty they steadied but the shadows in the far corners deepened. I hope they paid their light bill this month.

"What's going on?" I walked to the back of switches next to entrance to the men's room and used my index finger to flick one to the off position.

R.G. Crossley

A pot light directly over head went dark so I flicked the switch to the on position but the pot light didn't come back on. This can't be good.

Marne grunted. "That's what I thought."

"What?" Park's voice was tinged with fear.

Marne explained. "The storm knocked out the main transformer for the casino. The backup generators are beginning to have cascading failures."

She walked to the bottom of the stairs leading to the second floor. One hand rested on the polished brass rail running up both sides of the spiral staircase, the other had rested on the butt of her nine-millimeter Glock.

"I suggest we locate the chairman and hopefully he has a place we can hole up until the storm passes. We don't have much time before the casino goes dark."

I frowned. Some things she said made my alarm bells go off. Maybe it was the thriller writer in me, but I knew she was lying or, if not lying, she'd omitted a fact or two.

"Ummm, deputy, I have a couple of questions." Both eyebrows on Marne's forehead rose. Maybe I'm wrong but my sixth sense screamed at me I was about to enter dangerous waters.

She stared at me with one booted foot on the bottom step.

"If Simon's been murdered, and the roads are washed out, then it means the killer's still in the casino. And why would the chairman still be in his office at this hour?"

She moved her foot off the top step and turned to face me. Her fingers played with the butt of her pistol. Her brow wrinkled and her eyes were uncertain. It was as if she was wrestling with a decision.

She was making me nervous.

I ran my tongue over my dry lips and thought about that scotch waiting for me. Maybe I'd ask Art to make it a double.

A gunshot echoed from above punctuating the silence. It was then I realized the slot machines were silent, and the only people here were me, Park and Marne. I dove to the side of the staircase hoping to use it as a shield. I glanced at Park in time to see him collapse to his knees. His fingers covered a growing red blotch in the center of his chest and his eyes were wide with surprise.

A pitiful moan escaped his lips just as his eyes rolled up in his head. He fell forward to land face down on the carpet with a muffled thud. Like Simon, Park was stone cold dead.

Marne snorted. "Great. Why did he have to kill Parker?"

She shook her head then disappeared up the stairs. I was alone.

I'm a writer. The nature of my work makes me a solitary creature who only leaves his cave for food and water and, in my case, for visits with his friendly neighborhood bartender. Unfortunately, I don't think Art is serving this morning. Besides I may have had my last drink. I'd never felt as alone as I did right now.

Banks of lights winked out plunging most of the casino into darkness. Eerie shadows created by the remaining lights covered the walls, the slot machines and gaming tables. From where I lay on my belly next to the staircase I could see bolts of lightening flash across the ink black sky through the glass entrance doors.

I considered making a break for the entrance. I could sit in my car and lock the doors. But since I was one of only a few cars in the parking lot I'd be easy to find. Not a good idea. I shivered.

I froze when I heard voices drift from somewhere over my head. One had to be Marne's, but the other two were definitely male, and I definitely couldn't identify them.

I closed my eyes and willed my rapidly beating heart to slow. I had to clear my mind in order to think rationally. If this was a book, and I was the hero, how would I get out of this situation?

Think, dummy, think.

What were they after? No one just kills someone without a reason. Robbery, hate, love, rivalry, anger, for fun…these are all possible motives for murder. Unfortunately, sometimes there was no reason at all. Sometimes the killer explained it was just because they could, like the reason crazies climb mountains.

But in this case it had to be for a reason. Didn't Marne say something about a theft? And last week Simon told me he'd bought a rare and valuable manuscript at an estate sale. He said he was going to make some real coin, and finally be able to retire.

I shook my head. Simon probably told everyone who came into his store about the manuscript. He probably even showed it to a few people.

And Marne seemed to know it was Simon dead on the floor. Like she knows the name of a seventy-plus–year-old used book dealer? Yeah, sure a young, beautiful cop travels in the same social circles as a grey-haired book dealer? I don't think so.

I rose to my knees, then to a crouch, keeping my body as low as possible beside the staircase. Glancing over my shoulder I spotted a door marked EMPLOYEES ONLY. It's amazing what you don't see unless you have to. I'd never noticed that door before even though it was next to the entrance to the men's room.

It proves the urge to empty my bloated bladder is stronger than my observation skills. I made mental note of that fact. I could use it my next novel, if I ever write it that is. The sad fact is I haven't sold a book in two years. My bank account is nearly as exhausted as I am.

I kept a low profile as I ran to the door and stepped through into a dimly lit hallway. The battery powered emergency lights in the hallway cut the gloom, but there were still areas shrouded in darkness. I shivered. A bullet could end this escape at any moment. I paused and held my breath. Nothing happened. I'm good so far.

The hallway had two branches, one going to the left, the other to the right.

I mentally flipped a coin and went left. I wasn't sure what I was going to do, or where I was going, all I knew for sure is anywhere but the casino floor—or the parking lot—had to be safer than a room with two dead bodies.

As I walked I thought about Marne. The deputy knew me as well as Simon, but she knew me as my pseudonym, not my real name. I considered this and, since my books were out of print, the only conclusion had to be that she had been to Simon's store and seen my first book on the display stand on the counter.

My picture was on the jacket so she must have picked it up to look at it.

I was a lot younger in the picture, but I couldn't help but be flattered. A swollen ego is truly a terrible thing.

At the end of the hall I was met with another door. I tried the brass handle and found it unlocked. Good.

I opened the door to find stairs leading up into darkness. I considered going back to where I started but decided to press on.

Looking around I found a doorstop in the shadows. I opened the door and shoved the doorstop under the bottom to keep it open. What little light there was in the hallway would help me see the steps.

My stomach tightened as fear coursed through me. I took in a few deep breaths to steady my nerves and to stop my hands from shaking.

I'm a thriller writer, damn it. I write about serial killers and blood and death all the time. I had to get a grip or I'd never get out of this alive.

I opened my eyes and blew out a shaky breath then started up the stairs. The odor of lemons and garlic became stronger and stronger as I made my up the stairs. Finally I reached the last step and stopped and strained to listen for any sound. My heart beat rapidly in my ears.

I yelled as suddenly a bright light forced me to shut my eyes.

"Hey, Bert," said a very familiar voice. "Want the usual?"

Art. Art's involved? I licked my lips as the image of a glass of amber scotch filled my mind. "As a matter of fact, yes Art that would be welcome about now." I raised my hands to shield my eyes from the light. "Do you have to shine that light in my eyes?"

Art chuckled and the light dropped to the floor. I blinked to clear my sight and saw the vague outline of Marne, her hands on her hips, and Art holding a flashlight and a gun. The gun he pointed at me.

"You picked the wrong night to need a drink," Art said his voice bitter and harsh in my ears. My friendly neighborhood bartender was suddenly not so friendly.

"Listen, Art, whatever's going on here is none of my business. I don't know where the manuscript is—"

Stupid is as stupid does. Me and my big yap.

"Oh. So you know about the manuscript." Art glanced at Marne. "We should kill him," he said dispassionately.

"No. Not yet. He wouldn't like it." She paused and I worried she might change her mind. The next few seconds could be my last. Finally she added, "Let's take him to the chairman."

Art seemed disappointed to lower the barrel of the automatic. I had no idea he was so vicious. Sure he's a veteran, and had been in combat, but Iraq is a world away from the genteel streets of Lincoln City. I decided then to get a new bartender.

Art grins at me as he uses the gun like a pointer waving me to his left and then toward a door marked by the circle of white light from the flashlight. I stopped at the door and waited.

"Open it," said Marne.

I did and was surprised to find the office inside fully lit. The gun barrel poked my back to urge me forward so I stepped inside.

A large man with puffy, ruddy cheeks greeted us with a grunt, and dark sunglasses over his eyes sat behind a smoked glass desk. Covering his bulk was an expensive looking navy suit, with a dark blue shirt and maroon tie. His breathing was heavy and the odor of lemon and garlic was stronger than ever in here.

I winced when Art prodded me harder with the gun and I took a seat across the desk from the man who I assumed was the chairman.

Marne moved to stand by a potted palm tree in a corner of the office. Art went to stand next to the desk his hazel eyes watching me, the gun hanging at his right side, the barrel pointed at the floor.

"Mr. Acton?" said the large man his voice husky and thick. I nodded. What's the use it fighting it. The corners of the man's mouth turned up slightly. "My name is Barbas. I'm the chairman." He eased back in the leather executive chair and folded his sausage-sized fingers in his lap. "I'm a fan of your books," he explained, "which is why you're still alive." Another fan? I guess I'm more famous that I thought.

Barbas removed his sunglasses revealing one blue and one green eye. I'd just entered a James Bond movie.

He leaned closer to me and his strange eyes narrowed. "Tell me what you know about the manuscript."

He didn't say it but I hoped he meant if I told him he might let me live. These folks are obviously eliminating any possible connections to themselves.

"Uhhh, Well…" I struggled for the right words. Of course, being as nervous as virgin bride on her wedding night certainly didn't help. "Simon told me he had the manuscript, and that he bought it at an estate sale."

"Did he show it to you?" His brow wrinkled and I knew my next words would seal my fate.

I mentally flipped my last coin then shook my head. "No. I have no idea what the manuscript is, or who wrote it."

Barbas eased back in his chair and smiled. He glanced at Marne. "Good, he knows nothing. But he's seen us. Take him downstairs and dispose of him like the others."

My coin toss had come up dead.

Marne shrugged. "Ok, Mr. Chairman."

She uncrossed her arms and walked to stand over me. "Let's go."

I stood and, without looking back, we walked out the door. Marne closed it behind us leaving Art and the Chairman behind. Good riddance to bad news. It looked like good riddance to everything.

As we reached the top of the spiral staircase I muttered, "Dangerous waters."

"What?" said Marne.

"Outside," I indicated the entrance doors below us. Dawn was nearing and in the first light of day I could make out the angry whitecaps of giant waves pounding the shore in the distance. I glanced at Marne walking to my right, a step behind me, and realized her attention was on the doors. Now was my chance.

Pulling up before I took another step I stuck my foot out and Marne tripped over it. Her momentum carried her forward. Off balance, unable to control her fall, she rolled down the stairs with a cry of pain that abruptly ended when she landed in a heap at the bottom.

I raced down the stairs and dropped to my haunches then released her Glock from its holster. The gun was surprisingly heavy in my hand.

I heard an angry voice from above and without thinking pointed the gun into the darkness and fired. The muzzle flash blinded me for a few seconds, but I heard a cry of pain followed by a thump, which meant I'd hit the target.

I looked down at Marne and realized her neck was broken. Her eyes were open and her arms and legs were at unnatural angles.

The thud of heavy footsteps receding into the distance above my head meant the big man was heading for the hills. Let him go. Where is he going to run to in the middle of a winter storm in Lincoln City?

I decided to call it a day. Four bodies were enough for one day.

I raised my drink and made a toast to the dead. Thanks for the rotten memories. I downed the drink in one swallow then steeled myself to for the long march home in the driving rain and fierce winds outside these walls.

Dangerous waters breed dangerous times. At least it certainly did for four of my fellow humans.

About the Author

International selling author, Russ Crossley writes romance under the name R.G. Hart, mystery/suspense under the name R.G. Crossley, and science fiction and fantasy under his own. This year there will be re-issues the romantic comedies, Bachelorette: Zombie Edition by Champagne Books, and Antique Virgin by 53rd Street Publishing, paranormal romantic comedy, Zomopolis, and a new western romance entitled, The Fire In Their Hearts co-authored with R.S. Meger will be published in 2013 by Champagne Books. Also, look for another Aloha adventure, Bloody Betty Queen of the Pirates coming in the spring of 2013 from Champagne Books.

In addition the near future suspense novel, The Last Serial Killer by R.G. Crossley was recently released by 53rd Street Publishing in ebook and trade paperback versions.

He has sold several short stories that have appeared in anthologies from Pocket Books, St. Matins Press, at Smashwords, Amazon, and other e-retail sites.

With his wife, romance author R.S. Meger, he owns and operates a small press publishing company, 53rd Street Publishing. The company began in April 2011 and now has over one hundred e-book titles and a number of print titles, with more planned in 2012 and 2013.

He is a member of SF Canada and the Greater Vancouver Chapter of Romance Writers of America. He is also an alumni of the Oregon Coast Professional Fiction Writers Master Class taught by award winning author/editors, Kristine Katherine Rusch and Dean Wesley Smith.

To find a complete listing of his work check out his website http://www.rghart.com, http://russstory. blogspot.com.Razor's blog can be found at http://razorandedge.blogspot.com

Feel free to contact him on Facebook or Twitter. He loves to hear from readers

Other books by the Author

Titles as R.G. Crossley

Short Stories

Razor and Edge Mysteries
The Kidnapping of Billy Buttons
String of Pearls
Death by Clown
Beggin' For Murder
Ragged Ice
The Grand Central Mystery
A Strange Case of Undead Murder

Jazz Stiletto Mysteries
A Day Without Sunshine
Skullduggery

Non-Series Mysteries
Mirror Image
Dangerous Waters
Cape Disappointment
Boomerang
The Watcher of Wayburn Street
The Apprentice
Drip!
A Beautiful Friendship and The Parrot of Doom
Robine's Diary
The Christmas Club
Loose Ends
Splatter Pattern

It Takes Two

Anthologies
The Adventures of Razor and Edge:
Five Tales From The Quirky Detective Team

Novels
A Bad Case of Loyalty
The Last Serial Killer
Shear Murder

Titles as Russ Crossley

Novels
Attack of the Lushites

Short Stories
Countdown
Shoeless Moe
Round Up At The Burger Bar:
The Story of Trixie Pug, Parts 1, 2, 3, 4, 5, 6, 7
Five Minutes
Blossom Queen, Barbarian
The Secret
The Family Line
End of the Flies
With Death You Get the Eggroll
The Penguin Sleeps With The Fishes
Only The Worthy
Hero For A Day
End of Empire
Strange Bedfellows

Big Business
A Perfect Crime
The Wise Guy and The Pirates
In Search of the Perfect Cup
T.I.N. Men
The Legend of G and the Dragonettes
The Incredible Mr. Fix-It
Lock Stock and Barrel
Divided Loyalties
Cave of Wonders
A Family Empire
Until We Meet Again
Dragon Rising

Presents Anthology Series
Five Tales of Urban Fantasy
Five Tales of Bizarre Detectives
Five Tales of Mystery and Suspense
Five Tales of Weird Fantasy
Spies, Detectives, & Heroes
Tales of Twisted Crime
Five Tales of The Unexpected
Tales From Space
10 by Russ Crossley
Round Up At The Burger Bar: The Story of Trixie Pug,
Parts 1- 5 The Beginning
Worlds of Science Fiction and Fantasy
More Tales of Mystery and Suspense
Ladies of the Jolly Roger
Justice Served

Titles as R.G. Hart

Short Stories
Tikka's Big Day
"My Partner the Zombie" —
Hungry For Your Love Anthology
(St. Martin's Press)
Big Hairy Deal
One Red Shoe
A Bad Day in Lunden Texas
Hook Island
Grind Manor
Bloody Betty, Queen of the Pirates (coming soon from
Champagne Books)

Novels
Bachelorette: Zombie Edition
(from Champagne Books)
Antique Virgin
The Fire In Their Hearts
with R.S. Meger (coming soon from Champagne
Books)
Zomopolis